Dear Reader,

My mother loaned me my first Harlequin novels from the stash she kept beside her bed when I was still a teenager. When I married my own real-life hero, I gained a second mother, who also adored Harlequin Romances, and the opportunities for book recommendations expanded. During the tough times, I turned to these romances for comfort, or to be swept away for a little while. I also had fun reading them on Sunday afternoons, curled up on the couch with a cup of tea!

I am still and will always be a devoted romance reader, and I buy countless romance titles every year. What I love about Harlequin is that the stories have grown with the times, remaining vibrant and alive and identifiable as society, too, has grown and changed. A big round of applause to all

5

the folks who work to get our stories on the shelves month after month — thank you! And thanks to you, the readers. You are part of that special bond and friendship. May we move forward into the next phase with as much enjoyment as the last.

I hope you enjoy *To Love and To Cherish*. It's a story about a special relationship, too, between two people who have become rather dear to my heart. Perhaps you'll write to let me know what you think. I'd love to hear from you.

Jennie

To Love and
To Cherish

Jennie Adams

THORNDIKE
CHIVERS

This Large Print edition is published by Thorndike Press, Waterville, Maine, USA and by BBC Audiobooks Ltd, Bath, England.
Thorndike Press, a part of Gale, Cengage Learning.

The text of this Large Print edition is unabridged.
Other aspects of the book may vary from the original edition.
Set in 16 pt. Plantin.
Printed on permanent paper.

LIBRARY OF CONGRESS CATALOGING-IN-PUBLICATION DATA

Adams, Jennie.
    To love and to cherish / by Jennie Adams.
        p. cm. — (Thorndike Press large print gentle romance)
        ISBN-13: 978-1-4104-0964-5 (alk. paper)
        ISBN-10: 1-4104-0964-3 (alk. paper)
        1. Large type books. I. Title.
    PR3619.4.A327T6 2008
    823'.92—dc22   2008019226

BRITISH LIBRARY CATALOGUING-IN-PUBLICATION DATA AVAILABLE

Published in 2008 in the U.S. by arrangement with Harlequin Books S.A.
Published in 2009 in the U.K. by arrangement with Harlequin Enterprises II B.V.

U.K. Hardcover: 978 1 408 41239 8 (Chivers Large Print)
U.K. Softcover: 978 1 408 41240 4 (Camden Large Print)

Printed in the United States of America
1 2 3 4 5 6 7 12 11 10 09 08

For my friend June Monks,
with thanks for the
chats about life, the universe
and family. You are
proof that life can indeed
"Begin with C."

One day I may follow your
example and take up
line dancing too (but I'll have to
get fit first)!

CHAPTER ONE

'And stay there while I get the rest of your friends under control!' Tiffany Campbell left two goats on the correct side of her family's goat farm fence and headed off further into council-owned creek land to grab the remaining two strays.

Some of the farm's fencing could do with improving, but until her adoptive parents returned from France Tiffany would have to make do with shoring this section up. She wanted things to run smoothly while Colin and Sylvia were away. Wanted them to see they'd been right to trust her with the responsibility of running the farm in their absence. She could do this.

Not that she was trying to earn their approval or anything. She just liked to do a good job of whatever she tackled. For now, that meant keeping Campbell goats away from Reid land, whether the creek appealed to the goats this warm summer's day or not.

Arms pumping, bushman's hat rammed down hard over her corkscrew brown curls, Tiffany stomped on booted feet towards the animals.

She did her best to make her five-foot-and-one-quarter-of-an-inch frame appear large and intimidating. 'Hie, hie. Shoo. Towards the gate now, and I'll open it and let you both back through.'

One of the goats obligingly trotted forward.

'Good goat.' Tiffany opened the gate, and shut it again quickly once the goat had entered the paddock.

That left one goat, and Tiffany recognised this goat very well. She should, since she owned it. A personal acquisition bought in a fit of lonely insanity as it turned out.

'Right, Amalthea. I want you back in the paddock with the others.' Tiffany stepped forward.

With a loud *maaaa* and a look that seemed distrustful, disbelieving and decidedly goddess-like all at once, the goat bolted. Tiffany gave chase, but lost the nimble-footed creature when the goat disappeared around a bend in the creek.

Just beyond that bend stood the footbridge Jack Reid had always used to get from his place to hers. At least until her misguided actions had sent him clear out of Australia and to the other side of the world months ago.

Footsteps sounded on the bridge. Loud, stomping steps in a gait she would recognise anywhere. Tiffany froze to the spot in a mixture of hope and uncertainty. She had wanted a better resolution to her situation with Jack — a chance to truly deal with it rather than continuing to pretend everything was all right from opposite sides of the world. But was she ready to broach that resolution right now?

You'll just have to be ready, won't you?

'I didn't even know he was back from Switzerland.' Her muttered words indicated how far she and Jack had moved from their old, close and comfortable friendship. Would this sudden meeting make any difference to that? Maybe Jack hadn't even planned to see her during his visit here. Would he be sorry to have stumbled into her?

From somewhere nearby, the goat goddess let out a loud and annoyed bleat. A second later Amalthea trotted past Tiffany and disappeared into the brush.

Those swift human footsteps rounded the bend in the creek. And the time for questions ended — because there was Jack.

Solid, in the flesh, as wonderful and as gorgeous as ever. Tiffany wanted to see him only as best friend material — as he wanted to see her. Instead, her heart-rate picked up, her palms heated, and the skin on her arms and at the back of her neck began to prickle.

The reaction was embarrassing and unwelcome and infuriating. Hadn't she gained *any* ground since he'd left? She focused her efforts to ensure she revealed none of that unacceptable reaction when she spoke. 'Hello, Jack. This is a surprise.'

'Tiffany!' His head snapped up. Deep blue eyes churned with surprise, anger, and other emotions she couldn't define.

Fists clenched at his sides, Jack stopped in front of her. Muscles bunched in the tanned lean jaw, but something in his face softened, too. He clearly wasn't angry with her, as his stomping steps before he'd seen her had indicated. That left surprise, and that softening of his features. A warm feeling spread through her in response, despite all that had gone before.

'I thought I'd find you on the farm.' He spoke the words in that deep, delicious voice of his. 'I didn't expect to see you here.'

'But you did expect to see me?' At least that was a little hopeful . . .

'Yes. Maybe I should have let you know I was coming back into the country and . . . back here.' He hesitated and his mouth tightened. 'I phoned Mum from Sydney and arranged to visit her. Samuel was to be away on business for the next week, and I thought there'd be time to make plans with you once I'd settled into the house with Mum. Instead Samuel came back, and my visit ended half an hour after I got there.'

His tone was flat, but strong emotion lurked beneath the carefully composed words.

'I'm sorry, Jack.'

Samuel Reid was an often unpleasant man who appeared to share no warmth with his wife and was openly aggressive towards his son. Jack's mother was as bad, in her own way. She simply ignored life as much as she possibly could.

Tiffany kept her tone neutral as she went on. 'Samuel must have caught you by surprise. You don't usually give him a chance to try and launch into an altercation with you.'

'It was more than a war of words this time.' Jack's jaw worked before he shook his head. '*None* of the Reids are fit for family relations. *I* proved that today.'

Just as she began to gape at this pronouncement, he seemed to forcibly dismiss the topic.

'I came to the creek for a breather. I intended to seek you out at the farm after that. I want our old friendship back, Tiff. We're completely safe with that, and . . . I've missed you.'

It was an odd way for him to put things — as though he lumped himself in with his parents in terms of dysfunctionality in relationships. But Jack just wasn't like that. What had Samuel Reid said or done this time to upset him so?

Before she could think of a way to subtly pursue the topic, Jack spoke again.

'Tell me what you're up to here at the creek.' Dried twigs snapped beneath his booted feet as he stepped closer to her. 'I thought I saw a goat as I came over the bridge.'

'You probably did see a goat. I've had to retrieve several from this creek land, and there's still one to collect.' She inhaled the scents of dry grass and gum leaves, but mostly she was caught in the deep blue of Jack's eyes.

'I'll help you catch the goat,' he offered, 'and maybe then we can visit.'

It was brilliant that he wanted their friendship back. She should be on her knees and grateful for it, not disappointed in any way.

'That would be nice. I'd like to hear about your trip.' She would like a chance to resolve their issues, but she didn't say that. Instead, she tried to inject a teasing note into her voice. 'I was terribly jealous about all those fabulous places you'd get to visit across Europe while you consulted for your law firm. The photography opportunities alone would have been mind-blowing.'

'Actually, I got fairly busy once I reached Switzerland.' The smile he returned faded too quickly. 'I sort of dug in there and didn't move around as much as I might have. You'd have enjoyed taking photos, though. You're right about that.'

'It's great that Hobbs & Judd agreed to let you consult over there. You probably handled some big corporate law matters for them and raised their international profile exponentially.'

When he didn't say anything, she nodded her head. 'I won't ask you to confirm it. I know you wouldn't be able to give me information about what you worked on, but I imagine it would have presented a challenge to consult overseas that way.'

'It was something like that.' Again there appeared to be dark shadows in the blue of his eyes, but he forced words out in a hearty,

15

determined voice. 'It was a great opportunity to spread my wings, too — to look at the law from a different perspective for a while.'

Yes, and he had developed that yen for a different perspective right when she had revealed a personal interest in him. Oh, call it what it was: a *romantic* interest.

Clearly he still wanted her to believe his decision to go had had nothing to do with the fact she'd thrown herself at him. Maybe he thought if they didn't speak of it openly they could pretend it never happened.

Unfortunately, she couldn't forget that easily. But he was back, and he wanted to be friends again, and *that was good.* She nibbled on her lower lip. She would figure out how to deal with the rest.

Jack's sharp gaze followed the movement of her mouth before he abruptly looked away.

It was just as before. Something inside her warmed to that expression, decided it had a meaning quite opposite to what it really had. Well, this time she would take care not to be fooled by such thoughts. She pasted a bland, cheerful look on her face.

He gave her an odd look in return, but at least she had overcome her musings.

'It *is* good to see you, Tiff.' He reached

16

out with one arm and hugged her against his side.

It was a friendly hug, if guarded. It didn't matter that her head fitted against his shoulder perfectly, or that it felt like a kind of promise to be close to him like this.

That's all in your imagination, Tiffany Campbell, and you cannot afford to be hurt again, nor to take a wrong step and lose the return of friendship he's offered. So pull yourself together.

She wrapped her arm around his waist and briefly returned the hug, then forced herself to step away. There. See? She could do this. It just needed to be one step at a time. That was all.

Jack let go, too. Eyes narrowed, sooty black lashes concealing his expression, he searched the area around them. His voice was deep, husky, but the words were prosaic. 'Where do you think the goat might be hiding?'

While Jack looked away from her she took the chance to study him. The jeans and lace-up boots were his usual fare for when he wasn't at work in the city. The brown loose-fitting cotton shirt was not. He usually favoured fitted T-shirts. His hair was cropped shorter than she had ever seen it, too.

She hadn't taken it in until this moment, but now she did, and noted something that was more than a change in appearance alone. Jack had altered somehow on the inside. Because of what had happened between them, or because his life had moved on in ways she hadn't seen? She didn't know, but she sensed it. 'You seem different.'

'No. I haven't changed at all.' His head whipped round and his gaze latched onto hers, demanding she believe him. One hand rose to touch a spot beneath his arm, and dropped away as quickly.

Then he forced a smile, let his eyes crinkle at the corners and gestured towards her attire. 'I like that ensemble, though. It's got a nice "bush walker with cork hat" feel to it.'

What was that all about? Not his joke, but what had preceded it?

Slowly, she pushed her hat back. 'There are no corks hanging from this millinery masterpiece, and my shorts and hiking boots are sensible for this work.'

Both were boring as heck. But at least the T-shirt was pretty — bright pink and clingy, with little cap sleeves. Silly thoughts. She could be dressed in a wheat bag and it would make no difference, because Jack didn't see her that way. And he didn't really

18

care how she looked right now, either. She would swear he wanted to distract her attention away from his own appearance — except that made no sense.

His gaze lifted to her face and lingered there before he spoke in a deliberately teasing tone. 'You look like the same friend I missed all these months. Same knobbly knees and pointy chin and wild curly brown hair. Same freckles on your nose —'

'You can't see the hair. It's hidden under my corkless hat.' Had he truly missed her? His sporadic e-mails hadn't given that impression. 'And my knees aren't knobbly. They have character.'

'Knees with character. Yep, I can see that.' He nodded, let his gaze glint with a teasing light that was so familiar and dear.

Her breath caught in her throat.

When she didn't speak, Jack raised an eyebrow. 'Did you work at Fred's Fotos this morning? It's one of your usual mornings, isn't it?' He watched her with a steady gaze. If any shadow lurked there now, he kept it well hidden.

'I'm on holiday from Fred's to look after the farm while Mum and Dad visit France and other parts of Europe. They went over to pick up a cheese award, and they're having a bit of a break, as well.'

His brows rose. 'You're in charge of the farm while they're gone? It's a three-person operation with you helping out, as well, whenever you can. Have you got extra help? One of your brothers?'

'I can handle it. I won't disappoint Mum and Dad, and I don't need Jed, Cain or Alex to help me.' She never wanted to disappoint Colin and Sylvia. It wasn't the same as striving to please a birth mother for whom she would never be enough.

Besides, she was over all that old stuff — the worry of trying to be good enough. It had only been on her mind a little in past months because of the upset with Jack. *Everything* had gone off-kilter for a while after that.

And there was nothing wrong with wanting to ensure that Colin and Sylvia would be proud of her. Any well-balanced offspring would want that.

Yeah? What about parents loving their children simply because they were their children?

Well, naturally Tiffany believed that, too. But this topic wasn't even important right now. She forced her thoughts back to her discussion with Jack. 'Anyway, Ron's at the farm full time.'

The middle-aged worker provided all the

help she required. 'We made sure things were up to date before Mum and Dad left, and I can still make time to visit with you today. I'll just catch up later.'

'Let's deal with this goat problem, then.' He turned away, gave her a view of the back of his head, his strong neck and broad shoulders, and the way his ears sat close to his skull.

Jack was beautiful. She'd always known that, but over time she had come to feel it with her senses, too. Just staring into his eyes gave her shivers sometimes. Or if she looked at the way his mouth softened in kindness, or watched him interact with her brothers, her parents.

Tiffany had loved him since she was eight years old, and far more recently had started to *fall maybe a little in love with him.* Now she had to go back — to put those newer feelings behind her once and for all.

'Um, yes, let's get my goat rounded up. She's over there, watching us from behind that clump of bushes.' Tiffany pointed to Amalthea's hiding place. 'See the beady eye and the bit of white? That's her.'

'*Your* goat?' He glanced towards the goat's hiding place.

'Yes. I bought her to be my personal pet. Her name is Amalthea.' Tiffany watched the goat watch them, and thought about the many un-pet-like things Amalthea had done so far. 'To date it's been a rocky relationship.'

'Amalthea?' After a moment, he gave an almost reluctant smile. 'Ah, yes. That's the goat goddess who purportedly sustained Zeus with milk. I take it she acts like a goddess, too?'

Tiffany grimaced. 'She has come across as somewhat goddessy at times. Yes.'

A sulphur-crested cockatoo flew out of the branches of a eucalypt tree. It would have made a good 'In Flight' picture, but Tiffany had no time to think about photography right now. She turned back to face Jack.

He began to inch quietly to the right. 'You go left. We'll encourage the goat towards the gate. The first one of us near enough can open it to let her through.'

It took a bit of running. Tiffany uttered more than one stifled curse, while Jack seemed to welcome the physical activity. Eventually they got Amalthea back where she should be.

They stood there then, Tiffany and Jack, in front of the gate, facing each other. His body formed a half-cradle for hers, blocked her in against the gate, and she wanted to close the distance between them and have more than a friendly hug.

Did he realise how close they were? What if he knew his closeness still affected her in a way he didn't welcome?

'You could stay for dinner. It's nearly that time now.' Only after she'd issued the invitation did her thoughts go back to the last time she had invited him to her cottage for a meal.

Heat climbed into her cheeks and she hurried on. 'I've got Mexican rice left over in the fridge, or I could meet you somewhere else if you'd rather. You could invite your mother along, or we could just visit for a while now.'

'Tiff.' His hand closed over hers. Regret seemed to fill his eyes for a moment, before he let go and looked away. Then he straightened away from her completely, and she let out her breath in slow increments so he wouldn't notice she'd been holding it.

Jack's head tilted to the side. 'There's someone coming up the road towards your place.'

Tiffany heard only the pounding of her heart and the cacophony of regret and uncertainty. The sudden wail of a siren, when it came, made her jump. 'That's — it's turned in at the farm gate. They must have run the siren to warn us they were here. It sounded like an ambulance.'

'We need to see what's wrong.' Jack started to stride back towards the footbridge. 'My Jeep's parked behind the peppercorn trees. Let's go.'

When she didn't immediately follow, instead stood rooted to the spot as she tried to make it add up — ambulance, farm, someone hurt — Jack turned back. 'You said it's you and Ron. Would he still be here this late?'

'It's possible. He stayed to finish the hoof trimming so I could check the water troughs. We had some delays today that put us behind, and then I had to retrieve goats. I haven't heard him drive away.' She murmured the words, and as she did so injury scenarios began to play through her mind.

Quickly, she gathered the tools she'd used to try to fix the fence where the goats had got through, and hurried after Jack.

Once they were in his Jeep he swung the wheel and covered the distance to the farm gateway as quickly as possible. The Jeep barrelled up the lane.

Her breath came in sharp puffs, from a combination of concern and the effect of being near him. Nerves and confusion added to the mix.

The ambulance idled outside her parents'

empty house. The home was being painted, but with the painter gone there was no one to give directions. When Jack pulled alongside, the officers were about to get out of the vehicle.

Tiffany leaned her head out of the Jeep. 'It has to be Ron. He must have called from the phone in the shed.' She pointed. 'We'll follow you there.'

It took seconds only to arrive at the shed. Tiffany scrambled out of the Jeep. 'Ron? Ron! Where are you? What's happened?'

She hurried inside. Ron lay on the floor of the shed, his face ashen, one leg bent at an odd angle.

'We're here, Ron. It'll be all right.' Jack's reassurance came from right behind her, and his hand came to rest on her shoulder.

Tiffany registered the warm feeling of his touch and tried not to press back into it. 'What happened, Ron? I'm so sorry I wasn't with you.'

'I'd finished with the last of the goats and let them out of the holding pen. I was about to go home for the day.' Ron gritted the words out as the ambulance officers crouched to attend to him.

He cast one puzzled glance towards Jack. 'I knocked a hoof pick down and slipped on the dratted thing. Came down hard and sort

25

of twisted as I landed. I think I've broken my leg.'

After a swift examination, the ambulance officers concurred. Tiffany stood still as they questioned Ron, checked vitals, and quickly prepared him for the short journey to the ambulance. With a part of her mind she registered Jack still behind her, his touch a warm feeling of reassurance at her back as the ambulance officers loaded Ron so they could stretcher him to the ambulance.

She should focus on the *friendly experience* of Jack's touch, not the shimmery other feeling that coursed through her.

'Will you ring Denise for me, Tiff?' Ron gritted the question through clenched teeth.

His wife would need to know. Tiffany hurried forward to answer him, touched his arm with careful fingers. If it also offered an excuse for her to shift away from the temptation of Jack's touch, she refused to think about that fact.

Nor would she dwell on the bereft feeling she had now they were separated. 'I'll ring Denise straight away, Ron. Then I'll follow the ambulance in and make sure everything is okay for you.'

'No need. You should finish your visit with Jack. Didn't know he was back here . . .' Ron's voice wavered as the ambulance officers took him outside and loaded him into the back of the vehicle. His eyelids fluttered down.

'We need to get him into town.' One of the officers climbed in with Ron. The other closed them in and moved towards the front of the vehicle.

'Yes, of course.' Tiffany nodded and stepped back, and the ambulance drove off.

'They'll look after him.' Jack offered the assurance from beside her. 'And Denise will be there for him. But if you want to go in, we can.'

'No. That's okay. I think he'd rather not make too much of a fuss of this, but I'd better phone Denise and tell her the ambulance is on its way to town.' She hurried into the shed and picked the phone up off the floor. 'Ron must have knocked the phone down to use it.'

When she would have dialled the number, Jack laid his hand over hers. 'Tell Denise I'll be here to help you until your parents get back. Once Ron's well enough to think about it, he'll need to know that.'

'What? Mum and Dad aren't due back for ten days.' She started to shake her head. 'I can't possibly ask —'

'Then don't.' He squeezed her hand and let go. 'Don't ask, because I've already made

27

up my mind. Let me help you — spend the time with you. It will solve your staffing problem and give me what I want at the same time — a chance to spend enough time with you to really renew our friendship.'

'It's not that simple, Jack. You know —'

'I know my friend needs some help. Why wouldn't I give it to her?' His jaw jutted out, signalled his determination. 'I'm not due back to work for weeks yet. I'm free to help you. Let me.'

'You couldn't come here every day from the nearest motel, and I gather you won't be staying with your parents.' Clearly he and Samuel had locked horns enough that Jack would avoid the place now.

Milking started early on the dairy farm. Jack would have to be on the road before five a.m. — not to mention how she would cope with all that time in his presence after so long, with her thoughts and feelings all in a whirl.

'Your motel is in Ruffy's Crossing. It's an hour's drive away. And you can't stay at Mum and Dad's place because it's being painted.'

That only left one other choice — one which she felt certain he would reject.

'The only other option would be for you

28

to stay at the cottage with me for the duration. Obviously you won't want to do that.'

'Why not?' He narrowed his eyes at her. 'I've stayed there in the past. It will be just like old times.'

Just like old times? They would pretend the bit in between had never happened?

'Don't prevaricate, Tiff. You need help. If not me, it would have to be one of your brothers.' Jack touched the small of her back, a tiny guiding contact as he led her towards his Jeep. 'Let's go. I've got my travel bag on the back seat, with plenty of clothes that'll do to work in while I'm here.'

What other choice did she have? Call one of her brothers and let her whole family know she hadn't lasted more than a couple of days while she tried to run the farm alone? How would that look for living up to their faith in her?

'All right.' She tried to ignore the sensation of warmth that spread at the base of her spine from his touch. 'I accept your offer of help — as one friend to another.'

She just hoped she wasn't making a huge mistake. Because the next ten days could be a slice of that old, wonderful friendship, or be charged with the same unease she felt now.

Tiffany wasn't sure which it would be!

CHAPTER TWO

'We're almost done. There are only about fifty goats still out there in the waiting room.'

It was early morning. Jack made his observation as he rounded the corner of one row of the milking parlour and told himself things were working out just as he wanted. Better, in fact. Ron's accident was unfortunate, and he really felt for Tiffany's worker, but Jack hadn't expected to have a chance to spend so much quality time with Tiffany — and that, in and of itself, was a good thing.

Once they both began to relax into that time it would be really beneficial to their friendship.

He was here for that reason and nothing else. Last night had been uneasy, but that was to be expected. He'd kept the conversation on simple, uncomplicated topics — friendly topics. And if Tiff hadn't seemed entirely happy with that state of affairs — well, she would come to realise it was best.

Jack would make sure of that. Because he wanted his visit here to work out. He wanted her back in his life the way she had been before. Jack wanted that much of Tiffany more than he could let himself acknowledge, and he would have it.

There was no need to delve into aspects of the past that had no bearing now. The wrong path he'd started on with Tiffany before he went away. The Samuel factor. The other challenges Jack had faced in recent months. Jack had all of that stuff sorted.

He had missed Tiffany a lot. But as a friend, nothing more.

Right.

A snarl formed on his face, and he forced it away. The travelling yesterday must have frustrated him, or something. That was all.

'One more milking cycle will take care of it, then.' Tiffany rounded the corner from the opposite direction, and pulled up a millimetre short of stepping right into his arms.

Jack sucked in his breath and stepped abruptly backwards to avoid that direct contact. He resisted the urge to check that his thick shirt was correctly in place, and ran his fingers over his hair instead. 'I guess you didn't realise I was so close.'

'No. Sound distorts in here sometimes. I thought you were further away — in the next row.' Her pointy chin rose to a defensive angle. She stepped away and checked the flow of milk through the tubing that ran along the row. 'Actually, we won't be entirely finished with the milking when we're done here.'

She paused to tuck her overalls more firmly into her gumboots. Her T-shirt today was lemon, with tiny flowers designed onto it, her overalls a soft, mellow green. She wore no hat, and her hair looked soft and inviting where it sprang out from its loose ponytail. He had teased her yesterday, but in truth Tiffany was way too attractive — no matter what she dressed in.

Tiffany pulled a wry face. 'Amalthea avoided the milk shed again today, so it looks like I get to hand-milk her again.'

Jack drew his gaze away from the soft curvature of her arms, the halo of her hair. It shouldn't have been difficult to do so. 'You should have told me that goat was missing. I would have searched her out for you.'

The words were harsh, almost a growl. He clamped his mouth shut before anything else could come out, turned away, and tried to soften his tone to something a bit more normal. 'I'll help you find her later, if you like.'

'That's okay. I saw her hidden behind some hay bales in the south paddock. I doubt she will have moved.' Tiffany gave him a puzzled look and turned away. 'I'll get a bucket and take care of business later.'

They worked in silence for a few moments. The routine never changed. Check, regulate, ensure all the goats took the supplement, that they all appeared bright and in good health. This was good. Relaxed, normal.

Jack tried for some chitchat to cement that effect. 'How are your wildlife photos coming along? I noticed you've added quite a bit of material to your website.'

'Did you visit it while you were away? You e-mailed so irregularly I didn't think . . .' She trailed off and looked away.

Yes, Tiff. I visited the website almost every day. It gave me a connection, and I needed it. Even when I remained out of contact with you.

'I dropped by now and then. I liked the one of the goanna up on its hind legs, running up the middle of a dirt road.'

'Thanks. It was one of those lucky shots. I was toying with colour contrasts and a new zoom lens, caught movement, and realised the goanna was running towards me from a distance.'

Dust motes danced in beams of sunshine above her and his body tightened with an unwelcome interest.

Regret shifted inside him, and Jack battened it down. He had to look forward, not back. It was the only way to salvage anything. He pushed a smile to his face. 'It's my guess you got out of the goanna's way before it got too close?'

'Oh, yes.' She laughed. 'There's no shame in the judicious use of long-range photographic equipment.' Tiffany's laughter faded, but her expression remained warm, vulnerable. 'I got that shot on one of the treks Jan and I made last month.'

'Your watercolour friend from Sydney?' His heart soaked up the sound of her laughter.

'Yes. Jan got into her art about the same time I took up photography. She's fun to be around.'

As they finished up in the shed, Tiffany told him a little more about her most recent photography expeditions.

As she talked, they both began to relax. Jack didn't realise how much until they stepped outside into the morning light and stood side by side at the sink to wash up.

Then Tiffany's chatter died away. She glanced at him from the corner of her eye and her shoulders drew up into a tight line. All the ease left her. 'Jack — about that last night before you went away. And the days that led up to it. I need to tell you I truly thought —'

'You don't need to say anything. It was just a mistake, and it's finished with now.' He didn't look at her as he scrubbed up. The mistake was that he had allowed things to get so far in the first place, but he couldn't say that.

It wasn't a case of avoiding the issue, either. Jack understood *all* his issues perfectly well. He didn't have to burden Tiffany with the knowledge of them, though.

'Where did you and Jan go camping? Anywhere special?' *Talk about those things, Tiffany. Tell me how you spent your time while I was away.* He wanted to hear of positive things, upbeat things, to counterbalance his memories of struggle and difficulty.

She glared at him for a moment as she scrubbed up. Then she dried her hands and started towards the dairy building. 'What is special if it's not Australian bush land?'

In the paddocks around them goats bleated, drank water from the troughs and climbed anything not at ground level.

It was a natural scene, restful and calm, yet the air between them crackled with tension.

'My favourite trip recently was to Warrabah National Park.' She bit the words out as she stomped along. 'I got some good river-life shots there.'

'Great. That's great.' He realised he had moved too close to her side, and stepped sideways a bit.

The look she cast his way held frustration, but he just gestured towards the dairy.

'I'm no use to you in there.' The dairy was the one part of the farm Jack knew little about. 'How about if I load the truck for the next hay feed out?' He wasn't choosing to avoid her company. That would be pointless when he had come here expressly to seek it out.

He had irritated her, but maybe with some breathing space he would figure out how to keep her away from the topic of the past. He wanted to forget the last months, and that wasn't denial!

Tiffany blew a curl off her forehead, sighed, and turned away. 'That would be fine. Thank you for your help. I'll be busy here for two hours or more. You could also check the water troughs. And when you hear the truck arrive to collect the cheeses, would you come back to help load them? Mum prefers to have someone supervise each pick-up. That way I won't have to stop work.'

'No problem. I'll see to it when they arrive.' Jack strode away and attacked the hay bales. Throwing them onto the truck felt good, but only because it exercised his muscles in a satisfying way. He wasn't fed up. Nor did he feel in any way out of control or uptight or concerned that his plan to simply ease back into his friendship with Tiffany was perhaps not going to be as easy as he had hoped.

Jack attended to a half-dozen chores that included the cheese collection. When he and Tiffany joined up again it was almost lunch-time.

Tiff walked ahead of him to her cottage. Her bottom swayed beneath the green overalls. His gaze followed that gentle motion before his brain could catch up and remind him of the folly of doing so.

But it didn't have to mean anything. It could be just a typical male response. She looked highly attractive, that was all.

In baggy overalls that barely reveal her shape? Admit it — your memory and imagination are filling in the blanks. You're fantasising about her bottom.

Those thoughts were not welcome, either!

'What would you like?' Tiffany pushed the kitchen door open and paused to look over her shoulder at him.

Jack stopped his movement and whipped his gaze to her face. Heat stung the back of his neck and he couldn't look her in the eyes. 'Nothing. Pardon me? I wasn't thinking —'

'For lunch.' Small, capable fingers splayed over the doorframe. Hazel eyes bored into his. 'Would you like sandwiches? Eggs on toast? Soup?'

'Right. Lunch.' He forced himself forward again. 'Any of those would be fine. Let me wash up, and I'll help you get the meal ready.' He would do that whilst ignoring any memories or thoughts or anything else. She needed his help. He wanted her friendship back. That was the sum total of where the next ten days needed to take them.

They took turns to clean up in the laundry room. When he stepped into the kitchen to join her, the walls seemed to close around him. Memories he had managed to hold at bay last night hit him with full force now. Of Tiffany in a shimmery, clingy dress, the room backlit by candles, her hair a soft halo around her head.

Tiff had opened herself to him that night,

revealed her hopes and dreams, and he had turned away. But he hadn't wanted to hurt her.

Jack thought about Samuel, about the furious interchange yesterday, and the one prior to it, the same night Jack had come here to join Tiffany for dinner.

If he had realised sooner, he would never have allowed . . .

Well, it was too late now — in more ways than even just that. He rubbed at the numb spot beneath his arm and forced the memories away. *All* of the memories.

As Tiffany made sandwiches, Jack talked about some of the legal work he'd done while overseas. Nothing specific, just generalities to fill the silence, but her eyes shone with interest anyway. He soaked that interest up and hoarded it close — because at least he could have some things.

'Did you meet anyone really exciting overseas, Jack?' She set the plate of sandwiches in the middle of the table, sat, and took the glass of juice he'd poured for her.

They ate in silence for a few moments before she spoke again.

'Were there lots of business lunches and invitations to people's homes? Did you go to parties? How did you cope with the language differences?'

Mostly, he had just survived. But he wasn't about to say such a thing. He recalled something else instead, and smiled. 'One thing happened. I saw Campbell Cheeses in a delicatessen, and maybe I had a deep patriotic moment or something — I don't know — but I went totally ape and bought one of everything they had. It took me weeks to eat my way through just the varieties of feta with sun-dried tomato, and that was only the beginning.'

'I'm glad to know you helped improve our international profile.' She smiled, and even if it was a little bit forced her hazel eyes shone with warmth and affection for him.

He smiled back, and promised her silently that he would make this work.

All they needed was to focus on the truly important stuff and steer clear of the rest.

'What on earth?'

It was evening. Tiffany and Jack had done the last of the chores for the day. They were on their way to the cottage when they discovered a geyser shooting into the sky, near the tank that supplied water to her parents' house.

Tiffany gaped at the sight. This was the last thing she needed. 'We only started to top that tank up half an hour ago. It shouldn't have even needed to be checked until after dinnertime.'

'We have to get this contained before any more water gets wasted.'

Jack made the observation, and they both stepped forward in unison.

The water spurted straight up from a point in the pipe not far from its connection to the tank. Water levels in all the tanks were monitored, and the tanks filled from pipeline water as appropriate. Today, Tiffany had decided they should top this tank up.

'We'll have to stop the flow, then try to work out what's wrong.' Jack strode to the control source, and swore when he tried to turn it off. 'I can't shut it off.'

Tiffany turned for the machinery shed. 'I'll get a wrench.'

'It won't be any use.' Muscles flexed in Jack's back where the shirt stretched tight across his shoulders. He straightened. 'Something's given way inside. The mechanism's wrecked. I can feel it when I try to turn it.'

Tiffany forced her gaze away from Jack's back and her thoughts to the problem at hand. 'That's probably why the pipe burst open. Which means the flow isn't being regulated as it should be, either.'

Jack nodded. 'We'll have to do what we can to block the pipe, and then drive to the main and shut the water off there.'

'At least it's only this one pipeline.' She hurried back towards the spurt of water. 'It won't affect the water supply to the milking shed or the water troughs, and the cottage tank is already full.'

But the main was several kilometres away, further into the property, beyond all the groupings of work sheds, which meant they needed to do something about this right now.

A puddle already covered a large area of ground in every direction. Tiffany waded into the muck, gave thanks for her sensible boots even if the gumboots of this morning would have been better, and positioned herself on the non-geysering side of the water flow. Jack quickly joined her, and they examined the pipe more closely.

'We should be able to close it — or near to.' His blue eyes locked on hers. 'Have you got stockings at the cottage? Or anything else stretchy and long enough to tie around?'

'Um, I have some stockings, and a pair of black stretch leggings from when I went through my yoga phase two years ago.'

'Great.' He gave a sharp nod.

'I'll get them.' She hurried to the cottage,

helped herself to the required goods, and ran all the way back.

Slightly out of breath, she handed the items to Jack. 'How will we do this?'

He ran the pairs of stockings through his hands, seemed to realise what he had just done, and stopped abruptly. 'These are single legs. I thought they'd be put together already. I mean —'

'You mean pantyhose? I prefer thigh-highs.' And she had to muzzle herself right now, before she started to explain the pros and cons of ladies' personal undergarments. That really wouldn't be a good idea. 'What do you want me to do?'

He returned the Lycra leggings to her. 'Tie these around your waist for the moment. If we need them, we'll use them, but we'll try the stockings first.'

He positioned himself close to the pipe. 'We'll try to get the pipe mostly closed with the stockings. If that doesn't work, or if it's not enough, we'll go for the leggings, as well. I'll wind the first couple of layers around and then we'll take an end each and pull as hard as we can.'

It took a few futile attempts before they got the right angle and the right amount of pressure and managed to almost close the split in the pipe. By then Tiffany was soaked from crown to feet. Jack had fared a little better, but water dripped down his face and plastered one side of his shirt against him.

The moment he noticed her gaze on him there, he tugged the shirt away from his body in a movement that was almost protective. He turned away to gather up the couple of stockings they'd dropped in the mud in their haste as they tried to get the leak sealed. 'Hopefully what we've done will hold until we can reach the main and shut it off. We could have driven straight there, but a lot more water would have been lost that way.'

'I know. It was the right choice.' She turned towards the machinery shed where the farm vehicles were stored. 'We can go in the utility truck.'

Jack shook his head. 'I've got a full tool kit in the back of the Jeep. Let's get back to the cottage and take it. That way we'll have tools on hand if we run into any further troubles at the main.'

A fair enough idea. It would probably take just as long to assemble the right tools at the shed. But it struck her as odd when he told her to change her clothes at the cottage before they got in the Jeep.

Since an argument would waste more time, she did as he asked, but once they were in the Jeep and driving past all the sheds towards the main, she in a dry T-shirt and jeans and Jack in his existing jeans and a dry button-down shirt with yet more of the large front pockets that he seemed to favour these days, she pointed out the facts. 'We could have changed later. It's a warm day, no risk of getting a chill. Surely the water is more important?'

What was it with him and his shirt pockets, anyway? Had he suddenly taken to carrying around a barrage of goods with him or something? Not that she had seen any evidence of that since he arrived.

'It only took a minute, and I — I mean, you were very wet.' He didn't look at her, didn't change his tone of voice, didn't do anything but continue to drive ahead with his jaw clenched tight.

'There's the main.' Jack brought the Jeep to a stop and they climbed out.

They were able to shut it off without any difficulty. She wished she could shut off her concerns about them renewing their relationship as easily, but she couldn't. They drove back, cleaned up around the storage tank, and went on finally to the cottage.

Tension wrapped around them as they stepped inside. It showed in the way he masked his gaze as he looked at her. In the

45

elevated beat of her heart as she tried not to look too closely back.

To cover her discomfort, she said the first thing that came into her head. 'It really did surprise me to see you'd cut your hair so short. I never expected to find you with a military-style cut.'

'Everyone changes hairstyles from time to time. I told you — I haven't changed.' He almost growled the words, and shutters slapped down over his expression. 'Is there anything else you want done outside before we call it quits for the day?'

His attitude definitely was protective, guarded. She would even say perhaps secretive. Why? Did he think if he relaxed with her she would throw herself at him? Tiffany's eyes narrowed. Again, this was proof they needed a frank and open discussion to make things clear between them.

'There's always more to be done, but it can all wait until tomorrow.' It might not be what he wanted to hear, but she wouldn't make a workhorse out of him. There were limits, even when a person had volunteered to assist.

Jack dipped his head. 'I'll phone Denise, then. Ask how Ron got along today.'

Tiffany had wanted to broach an entirely different topic, but she nodded and turned away. It was important to hear how Ron was getting along. Things weren't exactly running smoothly around here so far, but despite the farm-related hiccups she still had hope that she could present her parents with a good overall result when they got back.

Try, try and try again. It was what she had done as a child with her birth mother, although nothing had ever been enough.

That was then. This is a completely different situation, and the only reason you care about it is because you naturally want to do a good job of things.

Right. And the situation with Jack was different again. She would figure out how to deal with that, too.

She set about preparing the meal.

Jack stepped back into the kitchen and declared that Ron was fine. 'Denise kept me talking with gossip for a few minutes.'

'She does like a bit of a chat. I'm glad to hear Ron is doing okay.'

After the strained silence interspersed with uneasy small talk that had comprised their dinner break Jack took first shower. Tiffany hurried through hers next, to get away from the too-enticing scent of his shampoo and soap. She stepped back into the house in her summer pyjamas with a satin robe tied over. Her hair hung in damp tendrils down her back.

In that first moment as she moved into the kitchen Jack paused from sipping his tea at the bench and looked at her as a man who was utterly aware of her.

She didn't mistake it or misread it. She was certain of that. As a result, shock coursed through her — shock, and a burst of unwelcome hope. Why did he look at her that way? She didn't understand.

Then Jack blinked, and there was nothing at all, and she doubted herself all over again. Maybe she'd made the whole thing up. It had happened before — much to her embarrassment.

Jack took a sip of his tea. He wore similar jeans and shirt to those he'd had on when they'd turned off the water main. A fitted shirt showed beneath. He obviously planned to sleep in that, and perhaps he had shorts or boxers on under the jeans.

Maybe she should have covered up in ten layers, too, but the thought hadn't occurred to her. She certainly wasn't trying to entice him, and her robe was perfectly acceptable, anyway. At least she had thought so until she'd surprised that look in his eyes.

Or imagined she'd surprised it.

His fingers tightened around the mug of

tea, and then he set it down and straightened away from the bench. 'It's getting late. I think I'll turn in. Goodnight.'

He started to walk away, past her, towards the enclosed veranda room that held her spare bed and opened onto the cottage's rear garden — an area comprised of mostly weeds and overgrown grass.

Tiffany almost let him go. But then it would just go on and on, wouldn't it? He had been here little over twenty-four hours, and in that time they had generated a great deal of tension between them.

If they wanted to rebuild a relaxed relationship, something had to be done about that — whether it made him uncomfortable or not. 'There's something I need to say before you go, and I don't want you to stop me.'

'Tiff—' His face a forbidding mask, he swung back towards her.

She went on quickly. 'Before you left I embarrassed you when I developed an interest you didn't return. To make matters worse I pursued the situation to a point where you chose to escape overseas to get away from me.'

Jack muttered an expletive beneath his breath. 'There's nothing to be gained —'

'Actually, there is,' she corrected him

gently. She wouldn't be swayed. They could put this off for ever, or sort it out now. In the interests of *trying* to get past all the rest of it, she chose now. 'I misread you, and I apologise, and I want you to know I won't ever project those kinds of feelings onto you again. I've realised they were a mistake and, like you, all I want now is for us to be able to move ahead as friends again.'

It was all she *could* want. And she would get her thoughts in line with it as quickly as possible.

Tension poured from Jack. He seemed to fight some inner battle before he finally gave a sharp nod. For the moment he seemed incapable of speech, but that was all right. At least the matter was out in the open, where they'd have half a chance to move beyond it.

Tiffany turned away, stepped towards her bedroom door and tugged it open. 'Good-night, Jack. I really am happy you're here. I've missed our friendship more than I can say.'

'Goodnight.' His voice was harsh.

He strode through the lounge room. A moment later the door to the veranda room slapped closed after him.

Tiffany stepped into her room and shut the door, then slumped against it. 'There —

see? That wasn't so hard.'

If she didn't count her embarrassment at having to address the issue, and the fact that those feelings she had just denied still simmered beneath the surface inside her.

Well, surely they would die away now that she had declared their futility so openly?

She climbed into bed and hoped that would turn out to be true. Some sleep would be good, too.

And then she tossed, and turned, and tossed some more.

CHAPTER THREE

'Eek!' The sound escaped Tiffany as a sudden scrabbling noise erupted in the lounge room chimney. With a shaking hand she put down her cup of herbal tea and froze into position, where she sat on the sofa.

A second later, something large and furry and agitated landed in a spray of soot in the empty fireplace, just steps away from her bare feet.

The room was almost completely dark. Tiffany could see only a shape — large, with eyes that glowed. She sort of — well, *shrieked,* and leapt onto the back of the lounge, where she proceeded to dance from foot to foot.

It was a totally understandable reaction. As though to confirm this fact, the animal ran right towards her, then scrabbled sideways into a corner of the room. When her heart started to beat again, Tiffany heard the slap as the veranda room door was shoved open.

A light flared from there. Jack stood silhouetted in the aperture for a split second before he rushed into the room.

'What's wrong? What's going on?' Questions flew from his lips as he strode across the room to her. 'Why are you up there? Why did you scream?'

'Jack — oh, Jack. I couldn't get to sleep, so I made herbal tea, and then that thing came down the chimney and it's as big as an elephant.'

Jack was another human being, a welcome sight, and instinctively she reached out her arms to him.

When Jack got close enough, she did the only sensible thing. She removed herself from the precarious safety of the sofa to something that was, in her opinion, far safer.

'Oomph.' Jack absorbed the sudden impact of her launch from sofa to his hold with just that one sound. His arms tightened around her and she clung on, her legs around his waist — which was as far away from the floor as she could get.

'I think it's a p-possum. You know I don't like rodents, Jack. Not without a lens and some distance between me and them. Not this close.' Her arms wrapped around his neck. She had to force herself not to squeeze tightly.

It was such a nice neck, too. Strong and firm, the skin smooth and warm.

Don't think about his neck or his skin or anything else like that. You have other problems right now. Possum problems.

'I'm sorry I jumped on you, but the possum startled me.' It had scared her silly, actually, and she still felt that way, but maybe she could brazen this out. 'Um, maybe if you could help me get to the kitchen? Then you could get rid of it?'

'All right. And possums are marsupials, actually.' He growled his response in a husky tone that inexplicably sent shivers down her spine.

'Well, yes. I know that.' For some reason his tone made her suddenly aware of the close press of their bodies, of the scant layers of clothing that separated them, of the warmth of Jack beneath his T-shirt and boxer shorts.

Drat it. She couldn't let herself do this again. It humiliated her to react to him when he didn't even notice she existed that way. She steeled herself for the short trip to the kitchen, at which point she would immediately step away from him and become utterly businesslike thereafter.

But Jack tilted his head, as though listening. 'Ah. I think I hear it now. Over there.'

He turned his head towards the scrabbling sound in the opposite corner of the room, and as he did so his whisker-roughened face brushed her upper chest.

Oh, wow. She sucked in her breath at *that* unexpected tactile experience.

Jack stilled completely. He wasn't even breathing.

That knowledge made her stop breathing, too, and somehow the tension shifted in a completely different way. What was happening here?

'You have to get down.' As he spoke the words, his arms tightened even more around her.

Well, yes. She knew that. She'd even suggested it. But first he had to get her to the kitchen. Preferably without the need to put her feet on any part of the same floor the possum occupied.

'In the kitchen . . .'

'Right.' He started in that direction. Almost reluctantly he looked into her eyes as he held her steady.

That was when she saw it. His eyes were dark pools filled with masculine awareness and interest. Even as she absorbed that fact — and it was fact, not fiction — his gaze dropped to her lips and lingered there.

'Jack?' A flurry of movement in her peripheral vision revealed the possum as it attempted to run up the wall beside the chimney.

Tiffany stiffened, but the possum scrambled down again, and headed back into the corner.

Jack walked them into the kitchen and shut the door behind them. She could get down now, but he made no attempt to release her, and she couldn't take her focus from his gaze.

He wanted to kiss her. The truth shone in his eyes, showed in the droop of heavy lids as he focused on her mouth.

With all thought suspended Tiffany could only feel. And what she felt was Jack. Her hand drifted from his shoulder, down over his collarbone, towards his chest. She wanted his heartbeat beneath her fingertips, wanted to know if it pounded as hers did right now. She wanted his kiss, even if she didn't understand it, and it didn't fit with what Jack had said he wanted.

'Don't.' The word passed between his suddenly compressed lips. Jack's fingers closed around her wrist to arrest the movement of her hand.

A second later she stood alone. Jack stood

on the opposite side of the kitchen and continued to back away from her even as he spoke.

'Stay there. I'll get rid of the possum.' He shut her into the room, shut himself out, and she stood there and tried to come to terms with what had just happened.

Chilled suddenly, she took a few dazed steps to her bedroom and drew her robe on, tied it. With a part of her mind she heard doors open and close, then Jack's low voice as he encouraged the possum to leave. Further scrabbling sounds, the outer veranda door being closed, then silence.

When she cracked the kitchen door open and looked around it she found . . . nothing. No possum. No Jack.

'Is the possum gone?'

She asked the question into the yawning silence. Only then did Jack step from the veranda room back into the lounge room. Jeans and the overshirt pulled on top of his sleep-shirt covered him from neck to ankle once again.

'Yes, the possum is gone.' He remained close to the veranda room doorway, as though concerned that if he came closer she would somehow contaminate him or something. 'It went willingly once I opened the outer veranda door, and it caught a glimpse of its normal environment out there.'

'Thank you for getting it to leave. I realise it's silly for me to be afraid, but I do prefer to enjoy my wild animals from a certain distance, and where they are happy in their own environment. I had the distinct feeling that possum was quite unhappy and might run up my leg.'

She used a deliberately calm tone, but her feelings on the inside didn't match it. Unwilling to prevaricate, she spoke of the thing she needed to understand the most. 'You almost kissed me just then. I didn't imagine it.'

His gaze became remote, forbidding. Utter denial hovered on his lips. She could see it there.

But eventually he pushed harsh words through his teeth. 'It was the middle of the night. I'd only just got to sleep. I heard you scream. You jumped into my arms wearing nothing more than a couple of scraps of satin. Any man would have been tempted. It was just a blip.'

'Oh, so it happened because of proximity and circumstance?' She narrowed her gaze as she searched his face for truth. 'Sort of like if you walked into a bakery and smelt a chocolate éclair, and you headed for it before you remembered you don't truly like chocolate éclairs?'

'You're not a *chocolate éclair*.' One hand raised above his head to grip the door lintel. Strain showed in every line of his body, in the carefully blank face. 'The reaction wasn't intentional, that's all. Now, it's late. We should get back to bed. I'll get up on the roof tomorrow and put some wire netting over the chimney hole so nothing else can come down it. I'll help you clean up in the morning, too. Goodnight.'

Ooh, the man made her want to scream. In genuine frustration, not possum-induced shock. But Jack had already turned away. Unless she decided to pursue him into the veranda room, Tiffany could only do the same.

But she wasn't happy. Jack was avoiding her all over the place, and he *had* reacted with awareness of her — which raised questions, drat him!

Tiffany spun on hcr heel and marched the few steps to her bedroom door. Once there, she shut herself into the room with more of a bang of the door than was probably strictly necessary.

Oh, she was grateful for the rescue from the possum, and for Jack's willingness to make sure the thing couldn't get into the house again. But as for the rest?

59

For someone so set on renewing a very platonic friendship, Jack had allowed himself to become quite distracted just now. And he'd been well and truly awake before that had happened, no matter what he said to the contrary.

It made her wonder if those other moments she had believed were all on her side hadn't been at all.

She now had more questions than before, and she wanted some answers — darn the man's attractive, confusing, irritating hide.

He should have stuck around long enough for her to get those answers.

Morning came before Tiffany was ready. She hadn't slept well for the rest of the night, but the farm work had to go on.

A protein start to the day seemed like a smart idea. At least then she would have something in her stomach other than aggravation and confusion and butterflies. Since when had Jack turned into Mr Secretive and Contradictory Man, anyway?

Because she was a good hostess, despite everything else, she headed for the veranda room to get Jack's opinion about the breakfast choices. Maybe he would be willing to discuss that, if nothing else.

Truly, Tiffany couldn't stop thinking

about what had happened last night. It had just seemed very real to her — more than a simple case of some sort of random and unanticipated hormonal reaction on Jack's part. She still wanted those answers. She intended to get them. She just wasn't certain how.

Jack was up and dressed. She'd caught sight of him as he'd moved through the kitchen when she had first got up herself. She stuck her head around the open door to the veranda room now, and spoke. 'I thought I might make bacon and eggs for breakfast — a bit of a treat to start the day right.'

He'd had his back to her. Now he swung around. Blue eyes glared, and his fingers clenched around something small that he held in his hand. The other hand reached for the travel bag on his bed and whipped the zipper shut, as though the secrets of the government, the FBI and world peace all depended on her not seeing the contents.

His gaze narrowed and words snapped out. 'I didn't know you were up.'

Oh, he was in a great mood. *Not.*

Well, guess what? She didn't feel particularly placatory right now, either. She wasn't a blasted spy, and what did he have to hide that was so all-fired important, anyway?

Another stupid two-pocketed shirt?

Did he truly want their friendship back? Because friends didn't jump through the roof any time the other person came near them. And, yes, okay, fine, she still found him attractive, but she would get that under control and it had nothing to do with this.

'I saw you pass through the kitchen earlier, so I thought I'd check what you wanted to eat.' *I didn't barge in, Jack. I knew you were dressed, and your door was wide-open, so think that one over.*

A glass of water sat on the bedside table, and he glanced at it before he turned a closed look towards her. 'No problem. And bacon and eggs would be fine. I'll be there in a minute.'

The subtext couldn't have been plainer.

He didn't want to acknowledge that he had overreacted to her presence, and he wanted her to leave the room.

You know what? Whatever! Her eyes narrowed and she turned away before he could see her annoyance.

To counteract that feeling, she started to hum beneath her breath. If it sounded more like a drone than happiness — well, too bad. At least she was trying. Which was more than she could say for Jack in certain ways right now.

It wasn't the best start to the day, but they got through their bacon and eggs. And if she remained inwardly grumpy, Jack, in contrast, now seemed to want to try really hard to simply get along.

But it wasn't simple, was it? Nothing was.

Even that one-armed hug he'd given her. Had he thought she would jump on him the first moment he let his guard down or something? Well, she had jumped last night, but that had been different — and, despite being aware of him, she wouldn't have done anything about that.

They went about the farm chores, and any hope she had of initiating a meaningful conversation slid into a black hole of near silence.

'That's it for the milking and storage.' Jack offered this piece of scintillating word-play after about two hours. He glanced one last time around the milking shed and nodded as though in approval.

They'd worked solidly, mixed tomorrow's supplement, and cleaned everything until it shone. But any two people could work side by side. What about actually managing to interact?

'Yes.' She snapped the word, and tried to tone down the aggression in the ones that followed. 'We've made good time.'

'Is there a cheese pick-up again today?' Jack dusted his hands off as though he didn't care at all about the tension.

Frankly, his attitude bothered her. Surely he didn't think this fraught interaction qualified as renewing their friendship? If he did, he might as well go back to Sydney right now and leave her to carry on without him. They could go back to e-mailing once every month or three. She didn't *need* his help here. She could manage without him.

Tiffany fought the urge to glare at him and realised she needed some breathing space — because other feelings bubbled, too, and she wasn't sure if she could trust herself with those feelings. She wasn't even sure exactly what they were.

'There's no pick-up, and I want to milk Amalthea before I get to work in the dairy.' Her voice still sounded more aggressive than it should. She tried to bring it back to a more neutral level. 'I'll put her on the portable machine today. It's a good first step towards getting her to milk in the shed with the others.'

'While you do that I'll get up on the cottage roof and cover the chimney.' Jack narrowed his sharp blue eyes and examined her for a long time, until she wanted to squirm or walk away from him.

Both, really. And how fair was that when he was the one giving out all sorts of weird signals? At least she only had one agenda. To try to be a true friend to Jack while she got all the other feelings eradicated from her system.

Well, that was her goal — even if she wasn't managing it very well right now. 'Thank you, Jack.'

In the spirit of that desire for friendship, and because she felt guilty for her aggravation even though some of it was deserved, she went on, 'I appreciate your help while Ron is sick. I could have managed, but it was good of you to offer.'

She just didn't get how his offer and the accompanying request to renew their old friendship correlated with his withdrawn and defensive manner.

'I want to help you. It gives me pleasure to do that.' He gave a short, sharp nod. 'Where can I get some mesh and a ladder?'

'There's some chicken mesh in the shed behind Mum and Dad's house, and you can take one of the painter's ladders.'

It was Jed who had suggested they get the house painted while their parents were away. It had seemed a great idea at the time, but now Tiffany half wished she had vetoed her brother's idea.

Then Jack could have slept at the house instead of at the cottage, and that whole almost-kiss episode wouldn't have happened last night.

Would she really have felt better about that, though?

'Right. I'll get to it, then. You'll be okay until I'm finished?' He stood there, dressed in another loose-fitting shirt and probably the same jeans as yesterday, wearing a closed and cautious expression.

And she could only wrestle with her thoughts, notice his attractiveness, and get mad at the world all over again. 'I'll be fine, thank you, Jack.'

Take a deep breath. Stay calm. Don't do or say anything you might regret. 'All I have to do is milk one goat. I'll be finished before you can blink. After all, hand-milking hasn't presented a problem, and the portable machine is a step up from that.'

Jack nodded and strode away to take care of business.

Tiffany watched him go, caught herself watching, and turned on her heel. If she didn't get herself together soon . . .

Well, some time doing something else would help her along.

She retrieved the portable milking machine from the shed. Now and then her parents used it on an ailing goat, or if for some other reason they didn't want to put a goat in with the others in the shed proper. Tiffany would use it on Amalthea as a great first step in her efforts to get the goat to milk in the regular way.

Frankly, she hadn't expected to have to milk Amalthea separately every day.

Pet her? Feed her vegetable scraps and other treats? Absolutely. But this disruption to the day's chores was a pain.

Even so, she would be kind to Amalthea — would win her over with soft words and a soothing attitude. And eventually the goat would calm down and take to being milked in the shed. Just like dealing with Jack, really. If Tiffany had patience, and didn't dwell on unanswerable questions, just tried to get along, it would have to get better — right?

So — okay. One calm, rational goat-milking experience coming right up. That would be a good start.

Fifteen minutes later Tiffany was beyond any attempt to make herself at one heart and spirit with her pet. One heart with Amalthea the hell-raising goat? Not possible!

She'd found the goat in one of the loafing sheds, enjoying the shade with a few of her pals. It should have been a simple thing to hook her up to the machine, right? Yet when Tiffany had tried to do just that what had happened? A stampede of one goat and one containment officer, that was what. They'd been chasing each other around the paddock ever since.

Dragging a milking machine over a bumpy paddock by its two wheels while a goat bolted away in front of her wasn't the way Tiffany wanted to spend the morning.

'Stop and let me milk you, for heaven's sake. Before you burst or turn yourself into curds and whey.'

The goat didn't stop, and Tiffany continued to give chase. She puffed and panted and hauled the milking machine along. Finally Amalthea headed towards the corner of the paddock that faced closest to Tiffany's cottage. If she could just get the goat boxed in there . . .

Maaa.

Amalthea bolted again. Tiffany, unfortunately, shouted some rather loud and disrespectful accusations about the goat's history, gene pool and possible involvement in occult practices as she hurried after her — just as Jack climbed down from the roof, where he must have enjoyed a possum's eye view of the entire proceedings.

That somehow increased Tiffany's annoyance. And made all their lack of progress in the friendship department rush back, too.

The goat ran towards the gate, towards Jack as he walked their way, although the fence still separated them.

Tiffany followed Amalthea. She didn't curse or run this time, and if Jack said one word . . .

At least Tiffany now had Amalthea so close she could visualise her hooked up to the machine. She needed only to grab her.

Tiffany reached out. Success was almost within her reach — until Amalthea rammed the machine with her head.

A well of battened-down feeling inside Tiffany gurgled and heated and frothed as she stared in disbelief at the goat. Her arms hurt from hauling the machine around. Her pride hurt because this goat was just too much. She eyed Amalthea, who eyed her back with no visible sign of remorse.

Finally Tiffany said, in a dark tone that boded nothing good, 'You are an Anglo-Nubian/Saanen cross. You're supposed to have a lovely sweet temperament and get your kicks out of climbing piles of hay bales. I can't believe you just did that.'

Jack chuckled. Right out loud. Right there in front of her. His eyes crinkled at the corners and amusement filled his face.

As though this were funny. As though he had nothing better to do than stand around and laugh while Tiffany struggled to get the stupid goat to consent to being milked. As though Tiffany wasn't already smarting — okay, fine, really *hurting* — from being rejected by him in terms of more than friendship, even if she tried to pretend it didn't matter to her.

Oh, she was over him in all but the actual outworking of complete physical uninterest, but that didn't mean she couldn't still be upset by him not being interested in her.

These stupid ongoing feelings that continued to pop up towards him were a pain, and they'd better disappear soon. And what if Jack *had* been interested in her before he'd left, like last night, and had let her take all the blame for it? What about that, huh?

'Ah, Tiff.' Another chuckle escaped Jack. 'You've no idea how much I needed that laugh.'

She only heard the word *laugh,* and she felt angry all over again. She was not here for Jack Reid's amusement, and she found nothing even slightly entertaining about the confused state of her emotions right now. She wanted to do a brilliant job of running the farm, too — and that wasn't exactly

70

working out at present, either.

Couldn't something go right for a change? 'Excuse me. I need to get to work in the dairy.'

Because that might not be enough of a hint for Jack, she forced herself to meet his gaze and tried to keep her expression neutral. She doubted she succeeded.

'I'd appreciate it if you could check all the water troughs while I do that.'

She turned her back on him. In dead silence, she pulled the machine to the gate and through it. Blast the goat, anyway. Blast Jack, too. She started to haul the machine to the dairy. Halfway there, Jack drew level with her.

'I couldn't help but hear your inventive . . . ah . . . descriptors for the goat.' His lips twitched again.

Tiffany set the machine aside and stepped into the outer room of the dairy. Funny how such calm could settle in when a person actually felt like a firecracker on a short fuse. She gritted her response between her teeth. 'I'll milk Amalthea later.'

When I've calmed down.

Tiffany didn't acknowledge anything else about Jack's comment. Instead, she scrubbed up and donned a coverall top and loose over-trousers over her jeans and shirt.

The hairnet came last. She snapped it onto her head with a twang while her irritation still burned inside her.

Go away, Jack. I've had enough, and you're no good in the dairy, anyway.

He guffawed, reached a hand towards her, burst into careless words. 'Oh, Tiff. You look like every mad scientist ever spawned in the movies.' His grin widened. 'You're so priceless.'

She should have laughed, too. Should have joined in with his mirth. Instead, months and months of hurt, that had absolutely nothing to do with this and everything to do with losing him, losing the hope of what they could have been, rose upward inside her like a geyser, mixed with all her confusion since he'd come back.

Jack wanted their friendship again. She valued that, too — so much — but she had wanted more, had thought they could *add something special* to that friendship. It hurt that he hadn't wanted the same thing, and it hurt that all he'd done since his return was keep her at a distance in one way or another, while acting as though everything were hunky-dory and A-okay, then confusing her utterly with random interspersions of awareness on his part that he quickly rejected.

Was that the best he could do?

Angry tears pricked her eyes, and a red haze appeared in front of her. She bit the tears back and pointed a shaking finger at him. 'Don't speak to me. Don't say another word.'

As the warning emerged, that fine line of control fell away from her. She felt it go, but couldn't do anything to stop what followed. While one hand gripped the door to the sterile cheese room, her words fell over each other in their determination to get out.

'I'm not in the mood to be laughed at, Jack. I feel embarrassed and confused and angry enough without you adding to it.'

'Hey. It's all right.' He took a step towards her, reached out a hand, all humour gone and with a look on his face — such a look. 'I didn't mean to be thoughtless. You made me laugh, and that felt so good, but I thought we were laughing together.'

A fine explanation. Thoroughly rational. Unfortunately, she'd lost rational somewhere back about round two of the paddock with Amalthea. Maybe earlier, if she were honest.

'I wish you'd leave me alone right now, Jack. But before you do I'll say the rest of what's on my mind. It's *not* all right.'

Her body trembled with the effort to suppress her feelings, but hurt and confusion and anger continued to well up. For a moment, the anger won.

'You're not even the same person any more. You're distant and secretive and jumpy, and you don't trust me near you. You reacted with suspicion when I walked in on you in your room while you tried to drink a glass of water, for goodness' sake! How dare you laugh at me, anyway?

'Don't you think I feel foolish enough because I threw myself at you and drove you away? Well, I *do* feel foolish. But you were there, Jack, and you've never admitted it but I wonder if you wanted me, too, back then? Just as you did last night. If that's true, then it was wrong of you to let me carry the guilt by myself all this time.'

Her body started to shake, but she didn't notice. She could only go on. Her words tumbled over each other. 'It's not fair for you to return and say you want our old friendship back, and then make achieving it so hard. It's not like the Jack I knew and respected and cared about to do that, either. And I don't get it. Do you hear me, Jack? I. Don't. Get. It.'

The words hung in the air between them. She stared at him. He stared back. Did he speak? Even now, when she needed him to say *something,* to respond instead of this stony silence? No.

She hated his silence. Hated it now, had hated it then. 'Oh, just go away, do.'

She pushed the door open and walked into the cheese room. Her temper hung in the balance. A huge ball of hurt waited beneath it to strip her to the bone when the anger finally left her.

Jack followed, paused in the doorway behind her. 'I'm sorry I laughed at you, Tiff. I'm really, really sorry.'

'No!' Just that word, all the way from the depths of her soul, with a mixture of all her feelings wrapped up in it.

Then — *splosh.* A stream of cheese curd arced through the air and hit him in the face, spattered his shoulders and chest and dripped slowly downward.

She looked at the empty vessel in her hands, then back up at Jack, and couldn't believe what she had done.

Even now the edges of the dam cracked, threatened to let a torrent of hurt through as anger made way for those other deep and painful feelings. Now she could add remorse to the mix, too — total and utter remorse, because she had never behaved in such a way. Never.

'Here. Let me wipe that off.' She whipped

75

her coverall top off and tried to dab at his chest with it.

Before she could touch him Jack's hand closed over hers like a vice. 'I can take care of the mess myself. I'll go and get cleaned up.'

He released her wrist slowly, as though concerned she might still try to touch him. Then he turned on his heel. The door closed between them and he was gone.

Leaving her with the echo of all she had said to him, spatters of cheese curd littering the floor at her feet, and confusion more rife than ever inside her.

CHAPTER FOUR

Jack bent over the bathroom sink and shampooed the muck out of his hair, washed his face and his upper body, and blocked his mind from assessing the scarring. It was no different from yesterday, or the day before that, or any other day for months and months and months. It would never change — and that had nothing to do with anything, anyway.

Bloody hell. For the first time in a very long time he'd laughed, really laughed, and he'd hurt Tiffany in the process. Not just today. He had hurt her the night he'd left, and since he came back, and he was only just now realising how much.

He dried off, buttoned a fresh shirt, made a mental note to toss some clothes through the washing machine soon, and yanked the door open. He had to fix this somehow. Although he wasn't sure just how.

'I'm sorry.' She stood right outside the

bathroom, her face a pale heart above the soft blue of her shirt. She'd removed the protective clothing. The shades of blue, both shirt and jeans, were a perfect foil for the rich brown of her hair.

Jack wanted to touch those curls, feel their softness between his fingers. Cup her head against his shoulder and beg her forgiveness. A part of him still wanted things with her that he couldn't have, too. He clenched his fists at his sides and sought for words that wouldn't come.

Tiffany went on. 'I can't believe I lost my temper like that. I had absolutely no right to act that way.'

'Didn't you?' He had to fight a sudden rise of emotion as he stared at her and faced, really faced, the harm he had caused her. His silence hadn't helped. It had hurt her all the more. But how could he broach the subject without revealing things that would best remain hidden? 'I don't know what to do to make this better, Tiff. Everything you said is right. You must loathe me. I wouldn't blame you.'

'No. I don't feel that way, but I am confused. You came back to renew our friendship, yet half the time you're so busy keeping me at a distance that friendship doesn't have a chance, and at other times . . .'

She stopped to draw a deep breath, and blew it out on a sigh. 'I blamed myself for imagining you reciprocated my interest before you left. I believed I drove you away when I revealed it. *Was* it just me, Jack?'

'It wasn't just you.' He didn't want to admit it, but her unhappiness gave him no choice. Jack tried to couch his explanation in the most careful terms. 'Before I went overseas I let us drift into something we shouldn't have. I'm as much responsible as you are, and I should have admitted that. At the time, I had . . . other things on my mind.'

His hand lifted towards the telltale spot beneath his arm, and he dropped it away with an internal growl. The two issues were separate. He needed only to explain what related to her questions here and now.

'Are you telling me you shared that interest but for some reason decided it was a mistake?' Her voice revealed shock, a residue of her earlier anger, confusion, and guardedness.

If she still owned any other feelings towards him she wasn't about to reveal them.

You shouldn't want her to, and you shouldn't feel anything like that, either. She probably feels nothing for you now but anger, anyway.

Easy to tell himself not to feel. Not so easy

to do. Especially when she stood before him and he wanted only to tug her into his arms, hold her close, and maybe take the kiss that had almost happened last night.

He had to be stronger than this. Not think of the way her body had softened into his when he'd held her.

So a residue of personal interest towards her remained? If ignored, it would go away. There was no other choice. 'I shouldn't have let myself feel that way about you.'

He didn't want to admit the bald truth that had upset him so much before he'd left her, but he had no choice but to do so now.

Jack took a deep breath. 'A part of me has always worried about being like Samuel — incapable of functioning normally within the intimacy of a . . . committed and . . . personal relationship. For a time I pushed those worries aside, but I know now I can't ignore them. I *am* like Samuel Reid.'

Jack had received not one blow to his life his last day here all those months ago, but two. However, it was his likeness to Samuel and his untenable behaviour that was the main problem, and that was what he would tell Tiffany.

'I can't risk inflicting that likeness onto anyone else.'

'You're not like him.' When he would have

80

argued, she held up her hand. 'I know it's worried you, but I've always said you're nothing like Samuel and I still say it. If you *were* like Samuel, how do you know you wouldn't hurt me as my friend, if you have that opinion about yourself?'

Jack closed the distance between them. Everything in him — every feeling, every emotion — reached for her. He let himself reach out in truth, too, but only to wrap his arm around her and draw her to his side, as he had done his first day back.

'I've heard people talk — people who knew him before he became a family man. He was fine before that.' Distant people, who no longer mixed with Samuel, but Jack had heard whispers years ago of how much Samuel had changed. How family life seemed to have poisoned him. 'Somehow intimacy brings out the worst in him. It does in me, too. I've proved that in my interactions with Samuel the last couple of times I've seen him.'

'You can't be right, Jack.' Disbelief crowded her words as she drew back from him. 'I don't believe this.'

'You've seen what he's like.' Jack refused to argue the point. 'Towards others he's irritable, loud, and at times obnoxious. But within his family Samuel's irritability becomes *instability*. He ignores Mum as thoroughly as she ignores him, and he treats me with aggression. Always. The only thing that prevents him from acting on that aggression is that I keep out of his way. The only reason he stopped being physically aggressive and switched to verbal abuse was your threat to him years ago.'

'I know that's all true. And I *would* have asked Mum and Dad to report him to the authorities, just as I threatened, if he had ever tried to physically harm you again.' She seemed shaken by his words, upset. 'But that's *Samuel. Not you.*'

'Is it? The last two times I've seen Samuel rage has overwhelmed not only him but me. I've wanted to throttle him — anything to make him stop speaking.' Jack clenched his teeth as he admitted it, but forced himself to go on. 'That's what a family relationship does to me. But, as my friend, you'll always be safe with me.'

He would have no hold over her. They wouldn't be tied to each other. And if he ever feared a loss of control towards her he could distance himself. There would be no commitment to stand in the way. Jack could be *committed* to their friendship. That was safe. But nothing else.

'I hope you believe me, Tiff.'

'I believe I'm safe with you in every circumstance.' She cast a concerned look towards him. 'If you lost control of your temper there must have been a good reason. It can't have been the same —'

'It was, and I've accepted that. I need you to believe it, too.' They couldn't afford to confuse this issue. It was decided, and that decision couldn't change.

Her chin dipped. 'I know *you* must believe it, Jack.'

'Then let's leave it at that. I should have explained earlier, and I'm sorry I didn't.' How he wished it could be different, but it wasn't. Now they needed to move on from this, put it behind them. 'I'm sorry I laughed when it wasn't funny just now, Tiff, and I know I handled things badly before I went away. I take full responsibility for both those things.'

He drew a slow breath, inhaled the scent of her, and tucked it away in a place he could keep it for ever. 'All I ask is a chance to be friends. It's the one thing that will make me happy.'

Because he couldn't do without that.

'I want you to be happy.' She straightened her shoulders. 'I think you must be mistaken somehow, about your self-control concerns, but I also believe we're both better off to focus on our friendship, so I guess it's the same goal in the end. Anything else is obviously not right for us, or we would both be determined to find a way to make it work, and we're not.'

Jack should be grateful for those words, for the knowledge that she no longer wanted to pursue a personal involvement with him beyond their friendship, and he would be. It just might take a little time for him to get that gratitude fully in place.

'Thank you for being honest with me, Jack. Now everything's out in the open between us, maybe we really will be able to focus on being great friends again.'

Everything? He couldn't hold her gaze. Instead he swallowed hard and looked away, because there was nothing else he needed to say, nothing relevant.

Jack turned back, dropped his chin in a tight nod. 'I look forward to that.'

The phone rang inside the cottage. After one long moment, when she searched his eyes and he stared back with his jaw clenched, she nodded, turned, and went inside.

Jack echoed that nod. It was time for life to move on for them — as it should have done from the day he returned.

■ ■ ■ ■

Tiffany moved towards the phone with her thoughts still on Jack and their conversation. It was good they'd cleared the air, but why would Jack believe such a dreadful thing about himself? There had to be a mistake.

What could have happened between him and Samuel to make Jack feel this way?

With a sigh, she picked up the phone. 'Hello?'

'Your goats are on my property!' The words were shouted down the telephone at her in an angry familiar voice. Samuel Reid's voice. It was almost as though her conversation with Jack had conjured the man.

'I'm sorry, Mr Reid.' Tiffany tried to sound concerned, placatory. She and Samuel held no affection for each other. She'd caught him trying to hit Jack with a riding crop the day they'd first met. But that wasn't the issue just at this moment.

Her repairs to the fence the other day mustn't have been adequate, despite her best efforts. 'I'll come and take care of the goats right away. This doesn't need to be a problem.'

'Oh, it's a problem. Those varmints are eating the bark off my prized stand of black wattle trees. I've every right to shoot them. Maybe I'll do just that.' Reid's voice vibrated with anger before he crashed the phone down at his end.

Tiffany held the phone slightly away from her ear and grimaced. She realised Jack was standing in the kitchen doorway and had no doubt heard her side of the conversation.

Jack stepped into the lounge room and stood beside her. Tension bracketed the sides of his mouth and his eyes were wary. 'What was that about?'

'Some of the goats have got into Samuel's wattle trees.' To offset the grimace that immediately filled Jack's face she pasted a smile onto her lips. 'I'll go get them, and then I'd better take a closer look at the section of fence that backs onto the creek property. I thought I'd fixed it well enough the other day, but apparently not.'

Jack turned back towards the kitchen door. 'I'll go. I don't want him to say anything to you. I don't want you exposed to his anger.'

Tiffany stared at his frozen, implacable features and relented. A little. 'If you don't want me to go alone, fine. We'll go together. But let's deal with this and get it over with.'

When Jack merely glared at her, she sighed and stepped past him and out of the cottage. 'Actually, it makes sense to take two of us to retrieve the goats. We can either take a farm vehicle or your Jeep. It's your choice.' It was. She simply wouldn't negotiate the point that they would both go. Not just Jack.

Emotions chased themselves across Jack's face. Frustration, annoyance, uncertainty. But in the end he dipped his head. 'We'll take the Jeep, but if Samuel is there, I want you to stay inside the vehicle and let me take care of things.'

Oh, really? She didn't deign to answer, and Jack's face became even grimmer.

They loaded up with a mallet, pliers, wire and other stuff they might need to fix the fence. It was a silent trip, but eventually the council creek land came into view. A minute later Samuel Reid's property line, the stand of wattle trees, and Samuel Reid himself, positioned beside a large four-wheel-drive vehicle, all panned out before them, too.

'There — to the right.' She pointed. 'I count six goats. That's not too bad.' It would be even better if they could remove them and leave quietly, but that might not be possible. Tiffany chewed her lower lip.

'Amalthea's there. Why doesn't that surprise me?'

Jack's gaze moved slowly from her mouth to her eyes in a grim sweep that somehow managed to convey restlessness and protectiveness all at once. 'Stay here. I'll tell him to leave us to it. Once he's gone, you can get out and help me.'

He got out of the Jeep and started forward — as though he actually expected her to obey this dictum from on high! Tiffany sat in stunned silence for a moment, before she blew out a huff of breath and quickly followed after him.

She joined Jack and pointed ahead of them. 'I guess that explains why the goats got as far as the wattle trees on Samuel's property.'

While Jack seared her with a look of disapproval, she examined the wide-open property gate ahead of them.

Actually, she was rather affronted by the sight. Samuel Reid had yelled at her about straying goats when his own gate gaped and invited anything on the outside to step right in and help itself.

'I know I'm to blame in the first place, but he could try to keep his gate shut.'

'Farm animals aren't supposed to roam on council land. That fact would be enough for him.' Jack shook his head and finally seemed to give in to the fact she intended to play her part in this. 'Let's just get the goats and get out of here.'

With nothing more than an all but imperceptible nod towards his father, Jack stalked to the stand of trees and herded the goats away from them, towards the gate.

Realising he didn't intend to even greet the older man, Tiffany hurriedly got in place to see that the goats moved in the right direction.

They all went through. Maybe the goats, even Amalthea, sensed Jack wasn't in the mood to be messed with. Whatever the case, she couldn't simply leave and not say a word to the older man. She realised she should have argued against Jack coming here. If being near the older man upset Jack, she should have arranged this so Jack didn't have to cross Samuel's path.

Now it was too late. But she could try to control the damage on all sides. 'Stay here, Jack. I'll just say sorry, and then we can go.'

It was her turn to walk off without him.

And Jack's turn to snarl and come with her anyway. She might have known he would be stubborn, as well.

'Good morning, Mr Reid.' She tried not to worry about Jack's bristling presence at her side, and called her words out as she walked steadily towards Reid senior. 'Sorry for the inconvenience. I'll make certain it doesn't happen again — although you could help with that by keeping your gate shut. From the grass that's grown up its sides, I gather it's stood open here for quite a while now?'

Reid stomped forward, and his gaze narrowed as he zeroed in on Jack, who stood silent and tense at her side.

Tiffany turned her head to glance at Jack's face. Oh, yes, he wasn't happy right now, but he certainly wasn't out of control or enraged, either.

'You've made your apologies, Tiff. Let's go.' Jack curled his fingers around her arm and gave a soft tug.

'Scared I'll talk out of school, Jack? You shouldn't be. I wouldn't want anyone to know what I heard you tell your mother the other day.' Samuel Reid turned aside. 'You never were much of a man, but at least you were whol—'

'The goats are off your property. I shouldn't have wasted my time. I thought Mum might want to know, but I was wrong.' Jack's expression darkened even further as he spoke over the top of the other man's words. 'Aside from that, the topic is private, and I expect you to remember that. Now, Tiffany has apologised, despite the fact you left your gate wide-open, and we're leaving. Goodbye.'

Father and son glared at each other. Samuel raised his chin to an arrogant angle. 'The gate stays open, and those goats better not show up here again. If they do, I will shoot them.'

'Try it, and it will be my pleasure to take the matter into court and throw the book at you.' Jack glared a moment longer, then made an angry sound in his throat and turned away.

Tiffany kept pace with his swift strides as they left the property. They collected the fence-mending materials, herded the goats over the footbridge, found the gap in the fence and put them back through it.

A few well-placed tugs and thumps and twists from arms that could wield a mallet and tighten a wire better than her, and the fence looked much stronger. *This* repair job wouldn't fail the next time a goat tested it.

Only then did they return to Jack's Jeep for the drive back to the farm. Samuel was long gone. Jack drove all the way to her cottage in forbidding silence.

When he stopped the Jeep, she turned to him. 'You're nothing like him —'

'Do you see now, Tiffany? I could feel my anger building again, just like the last time —' Jack spoke at the same time, and broke off abruptly.

There was something here — something that just wasn't quite right. Tiffany tried to puzzle it out, but couldn't put the pieces together. She only came up with one thing. 'What did he mean, Jack? Was it to do with your concerns about being like him? Maybe if you tell me, you'll feel better?'

Samuel had to be striking out at Jack in areas that really upset him. Nothing else could explain Jack becoming so overly upset, and that was still a far cry from uncontrolled rage.

'I've already explained my feelings about my family gene pool.' Back straight, Jack faced her, willed her agreement with deep blue eyes. 'There's nothing else to say.'

'All right. I respect your feelings.' She just didn't agree with them, that was all.

CHAPTER FIVE

For the next couple of days Tiffany and Jack worked together in relative harmony — and worked hard to restore their friendship.

Despite various uncertainties, Tiffany did begin to sew her trust into that friendship again. Maybe she shouldn't worry about things all over the place.

Just because Jack had moved on to a different style of clothing, had cut his hair short and seemed a bit jumpy in the mornings, and obsessed about covering himself up, it didn't have to mean anything.

She wished she could convince him he wasn't like his father, but, that aside, he had made what he now wanted from her clear. She had to move on, as well. And if the occasional twinge of reaction to him still happened, she was doing her best to stamp out said reaction.

'It's all good, and if this rotten stuffy weather would quit, life would be practically perfect,' she said aloud. An exaggeration, perhaps, but in the interests of a cooler cottage later tonight, Tiffany wanted to throw the windows open to let in any late-afternoon breeze that might come along.

Maybe she should change out of her jeans and into shorts, even if Jack did think she had knobbly knees.

In fact, a wind had sprung up, so maybe the weather was about to turn. Admittedly it was a blustery, warm wind at this stage, but that could change.

She decided against the shorts for now, and instead pushed open the window in her bedroom and moved through the cottage to open a couple of windows in the veranda room, as well. If she left the door to the veranda room open, too, any breeze should draw right through.

Jack was at the tank near her parents' house. After they'd spoken with her parents by phone last night, they had called a local plumber to work on the water feed from that pipeline, and Jack had volunteered to help when the guy arrived.

No doubt Jack was still there, his muscles bulging as he helped with the physical work.

Which is why I'm in here, far away from those muscles. I'm minding my own business while I get those inappropriate thoughts under control.

You continue to believe that.

'It's *true*.' She huffed out the words and stole a glance towards the bed where Jack lay each night, where she had visualised him while she lay awake in her room and stared at the ceiling. 'Okay. Maybe it's not as simple as I might like it to be, but I'll get there.'

Jack's travel bag sat unzipped at the foot of the bed. She told herself to respect his privacy and not look, but in that one glance something unexpected caught her eye.

A bottle of pills was tucked half away, beside a neatly folded shirt. Jack didn't generally take medication, and something about this bottle looked somehow familiar. Tiffany paused, her gaze on the bottle, brows drawn together as inexplicable unease began to grow inside her.

It's not your business.

But Jack rarely took even a paracetamol, unless he absolutely couldn't avoid it, and these were clearly prescription. The other morning flashed through her mind again. The glass of water, his hand clenched over something, the secretiveness that she had tried to dismiss in the days since then.

Tablets. He'd been taking tablets. And he

hadn't wanted her to see him do so.

Samuel Reid's taunt towards Jack came back, too.

I wouldn't want anyone to know what I heard you tell your mother . . . You never were much of a man . . .

Was Jack in some sort of trouble? Ill? He looked perfectly well. She picked up the bottle, read the label — and remembered. She'd watched a documentary that mentioned this medication on TV weeks ago.

But the medication must be used for other things!

Above everything, Tiffany wanted to believe that. But she couldn't. Because too many things now cascaded through her mind, one after another, threatening to shut her thoughts down completely.

Jack hadn't changed his hairstyle. Not by choice. He hadn't just decided to wear loose-fitting shirts, either. He was hiding something under those shirts. Hence the one-armed hugs that she'd thought were a warning to stick to 'friendly'.

Maybe they had been, but they were something else, too. Something far more devastating. And he hadn't cut his hair. It had fallen out and was now growing back.

'Oh, God. Oh, God.' Sick fear swept over her, through her. The fingers that held the bottle started to tremble, and she turned to hide the tablets back in Jack's bag.

Where she could forget they existed? Refuse to think about what they meant? She didn't know — couldn't think.

'What the hell are you doing?' Jack's low, accusing tone came from right behind her.

She swung round, faced the fury of his expression, the face that had paled beneath his tan as his desperate blue gaze flicked from the bottle in her hand to her face and back again.

'I — I decided to open all the windows to help air the cottage out. It's been so h-hot.' She took one step towards him. Her heart was filled with fear. Nausea clawed at her insides. 'The bag was open. I didn't open the bag, Jack. The tablets were right there, and I saw them and I was scared. Samuel knows, doesn't he? That's why you got enraged. It's not the same thing — don't you see?'

The words babbled out of her.

Jack's fists clenched and unclenched at his sides. Anger and frustration and pain and regret warred in his features as he stood in the doorway of the room.

When he spoke, his voice was a low growl of sound that rasped over her nerve-endings. 'This wasn't your business, Tiffany. You were never meant to know.'

'I *have* to know. Are you all right? What happened to you? When did it happen? Are you . . . okay now?' The questions poured straight from her heart, straight from the well of fear for him that grew and grew.

What did he mean, she was never meant to know? She was so confused.

Jack stepped forward then, right into the room, and took the bottle from her grip. He tossed it back into the bag and zipped it shut. His movements were jerky, his jaw clenched into one big bunch of strained muscle. 'They're just some tablets —'

'No, they're not. Don't try to hide this. It's way too late, and I've had enough of your secrets!' Tears burned at the backs of her eyes as reality crashed over her. She blinked them back fiercely.

'The active ingredient in that medication —' her hand trembled as she pointed towards his now closed bag '— is used for patients as part of post-operative c-cancer treatment.'

She struggled to force the words from between her lips. 'I saw the same pills in a documentary. They said how good the pills were. Less side effects. I *saw* it, Jack, so don't try to deny this.'

While Jack growled out a low oath, a

shudder started at her feet and consumed her. Somehow she got her hands onto him, fingers clasped around his forearms. It seemed vital to have hold of him, to assure herself he was here, upright, breathing, *okay.*

A cold fury had built in Jack's eyes, but she couldn't think about that. 'What happened to you, Jack? You have to tell me.'

'All right. It's true.' Jack all but snarled the words out of his frustration — because Tiffany should never have known this. It wasn't anything else but that very understandable feeling.

If he had to work to resist the urge to start smashing things in the room, if he felt uptight and uncertain inside, that was simply a result of his understandable disturbance.

She was never to have known, but now she did. And the knowledge had filled her with fear and anguish, just as he had known it would. *That* fact was worth getting upset about. And all this was a total waste. Her knowing changed nothing, helped nothing. It simply complicated things.

He wanted to refuse to speak of it, to ignore her discovery. Not because he couldn't deal with what she might think. He'd had the counselling sessions before and after the surgery and the treatment —

yada, yada, yada. He knew he had no reason to feel less of a person. No matter what Samuel might have said to the contrary.

Jack's jaw clenched. Naturally he was over all that crap. But it didn't mean he wanted to spill his guts to Tiffany. Nor that knowing about this was best for her. It wasn't.

But she knew now, and he had to control the damage and get her past this. 'All right, you've worked it out. I've had cancer. The operative word is *had.* The episode is in the past, so you don't need to worry about it.'

'Was it — was it lung cancer?' Her glance dropped to his chest. The concern in her eyes didn't diminish. 'The loose shirts . . . does it still hurt you?'

'No.' It didn't hurt at all — not physically, and not emotionally or mentally, either. He never even thought about it nowadays. That was fine, too, because there was nothing to think about, nothing he could change. So why waste any brain space on it? Like he said, totally over it.

'I had abs cancer, male breast cancer, on the left side. The lump was a couple of inches above my top rib.' His hand rose to cover the scar site.

There. He'd said it, and the sky hadn't fallen in. See? No problem. He dropped his hand away.

Wide hazel eyes clung to his face. 'But when? How? You never said anything. My God, Jack. You could have died and I didn't even know!'

'I found the lump a month before I went overseas.'

Jack had discovered the problem right when the two of them had begun to relate to each other in a different way, to consider something beyond friendship. He had ignored the small bump, thought nothing of it.

'I didn't think it was serious, but when it didn't go away I decided to get it checked out.'

'Jack . . .' Tiffany's face was tight, her eyes overbright. She looked on the edge of desperation.

'As far as any person can know, I should now fully recover. The pills are to help with that process, that's all.' The summary had skipped several chapters. He knew it. But he wanted her to let the topic drop.

He even started to turn away, with some idea of leaving, getting on with some work or something. Her hand on his arm stopped him, the grip of her fingers surprisingly strong.

His gaze swung to hers. He caught pain in her eyes, ongoing concern, and a beginning swell of something that looked like anger. He let his gaze move to the opened windows and beyond, to the sky. There were dark clouds on the horizon that seemed to well up inside the room, too.

She dropped her hand away from him. 'When did you go to the doctor, Jack? When did you find out what was wrong?'

'I found out the results the day I told you I intended to go overseas.' The timing had been incidental, and he had to make that clear. 'I *did* work while I was there. I *did* set it up with my firm so I could consult for them there, and I *did* choose to put some distance between you and me because I'd realised I was too like Samuel to safely pursue that kind of relationship with you or with anyone else. All those things were true.'

In fact, he'd had a vicious episode with Samuel before he'd seen Tiffany that night. One that had struck him on the raw when he had only just learned of his condition, and had brought home to him the truth that the same evil Samuel displayed towards him was there in Jack, too.

'Samuel taunted me that afternoon. It was a stupid attack, but I flew at him, Tiff.'

Her mouth pulled into a defensive line. 'You would have been upset. You'd just had terrible news —'

'Upset enough to bodily charge at him? He didn't know the news I'd received.'

But Samuel had somehow perceived the change in Jack's attitude to Tiffany. And when the older man had said Jack was a fool to think of getting involved with Tiffany, Jack hadn't wanted to accept it.

Well, Samuel had got the reaction he'd set out to get.

'I made myself walk away. Then I came to you, and I knew I could never risk hurting you that way. I'd already decided to have my treatment overseas. I realised then that I had to draw back from you personally, too — let things cool off between us. That's why I didn't tell you my plans. You'd have wanted to be part of them, and that wasn't the right choice.'

'In fact, you had the whole thing tidied up nicely.' Tiffany made the observation in a tight voice, but it was the best she could manage. 'If only you had told me, let me —'

She stumbled to a stop. Her best friend had suffered a life-threatening illness and hadn't even told her about it. How did she articulate that?

He had never wanted her to know about this at all. That knowledge hurt. But now she did know, and she was scared, and she was beginning to be a lot of other things, too.

Jack had stepped back from a personal closeness with her because he'd come to believe he was like Samuel. That was sad, and she still hoped she could find some way to make him see it wasn't true, but he had stepped back from her in a much more elemental way, by choosing to hide his cancer from her. In fact, he had robbed her of all choice in the matter.

Hurt washed through her in a swift, tidal sweep that mingled with other feelings to form a foaming, terrifying mass.

'Why would you shut me out like that?' Her pain and confusion were in her voice. She sought his gaze, but he looked away.

Instead, he lifted his hand, jammed it through the telltale short hair. His other hand had dropped away from its position above his heart, but what had that earlier protective gesture signified about his mental and emotional state?

'I didn't shut you out.' Even his denial rang hollow. 'I made a choice to have my treatment privately, and I realised we couldn't go on the way we were. I took steps to correct that, too. It all happened in a tight timeframe, that's all.'

Wind buffeted the outside of the cottage,

grew in strength and seemed to match Tiffany's mood. She ignored the sudden darkening of the room as clouds obscured the sun. Instead she kept her attention on Jack. 'And you made all the decisions for both of us.'

'It was my issue. I wanted to protect you from upset, Tiff.' He took a step towards her, then stopped. 'When you came to Colin and Sylvia you'd had so much worry and fear in your life. It made you tough on the outside, but you were vulnerable on the inside, and I know you haven't ever completely overcome that vulnerability. I refused to let you worry about me and you would have — would have suffered as a result.'

'I am not vulnerable.' Did he think her some sort of wimp? 'And who made *you* the judge of what I can or cannot face, anyway?'

She pushed aside the twinge that suggested maybe she did still carry some baggage around, maybe she did worry a little too much about pleasing other people. Yes, of course she would have felt uptight on Jack's behalf, but there was nothing odd about that!

'I was your best friend, Jack.' That was what mattered in all of this. 'Even if you didn't want anything else from me, don't you think I had the right to be there for you if I wanted to? As your friend?'

Yes, she would have been afraid for him — desperately afraid. Those fears gripped her now, and Tiffany had to deal with them. Fear of what might have happened to him. Fear that it might somehow come back. She had the right to own those fears.

'You locked me out at every step, Jack. Can you imagine how that makes me feel?'

'Tiffany.' Jack swore, a soft curse beneath his breath, filled with emotion. He stepped forward, reached out his arms.

Would he give her a one-sided hug, then pat her on the head and set her away from him again? A part of her wanted nothing more than to be physically close, but she wanted real closeness. To wrap her arms around him all the way from front to back, to hold on to him and be assured he was well.

But Jack stopped, and she remained still. If he had offered less than that, she couldn't have taken it. Not right now.

Words burst out. 'You didn't let me be there for you, Jack. Not to share the uncertainty. Not to stand at your side and help you. Not even just to know, to bear the knowledge with you. Despite all the ways you have locked me out — not just then, but since you came back here, too — I can't comprehend how you could withhold something so important from me. Maybe I should be able to do that. Maybe I should feel used to that by now. But I'm not, Jack. I'm not used to it.'

'I'm sorry if I hurt you. But I told you my reasons. They were for you, for your sake.' On his face was torture.

It felt odd to look at him and see what she felt inside herself. In that moment Tiffany knew she couldn't hear Jack offer those reasons again.

They weren't good enough. Nothing could be good enough. 'You haven't trusted me from the start. Not even a little. Not at all.'

'That's not true.' Jack spoke the words, but doubt revealed itself in his gaze. 'This wasn't about trust. I had to protect you. Please understand —'

'No, Jack. I don't understand.' Tiffany turned blindly away. She hesitated outside her room, grabbed something from inside it, and walked out of the house.

Jack didn't see what Tiffany held in her hands, but he watched her stiff back as she walked away. Perhaps it was best. She needed time to absorb the information, and then she would come to realise he'd spoken the truth. She would sort through his reasons, why he had drawn back from her and kept the cancer from her. She would see all those choices were right, were best for her.

She was all that mattered, and if he still cared for her in ways he could never admit that was irrelevant. He wanted her friendship. He could have that. It was all he could have.

If other ideas beckoned, filled him sometimes, they were impossible. And Jack needed to treat them as such.

CHAPTER SIX

Storm clouds gathered over the small reserve where the council creek land opened out into a stand of gum trees that surrounded a natural billabong. The water was low, but there were kangaroos there right now, cropping grass beside the brackish water.

Tiffany had no idea why she had snatched up her camera as she'd left the cottage. Maybe because photography had provided a panacea after Jack went away. She could certainly do with some kind of calming effect now.

The largest kangaroo lifted its head and aimed an arrogant glance towards one of the other, smaller animals when it dared to get too close. Tiffany clicked off several pictures and admitted she felt somewhat aggressive herself right now. She could blame it on the swirl of the grey sky, on the rampant, threatening cloud formations, but she didn't.

Her anger was all about Jack, and had been for the past hour as she had worked to come to terms with all he had told her.

Click, click, click.

She snapped photographs while hurt swirled like those dark clouds above. The anger was the easy part.

'He shut me out as though all those years of closeness didn't even matter.'

Click, click, click.

Thunder rumbled and the kangaroos melted away among the trees. Tiffany turned her camera up to the sky and continued to shoot.

Click, click, click.

'What kind of friendship can't withstand its first real difficulty? It's those times when friends do the most, and they do it because they want to!'

She snapped off shots, each one darker and more tumultuous than the last. Actually, the one of the dead tree with its forked branches that reached straight up towards a black sky wasn't bad. Maybe she would frame it and hang it in the cottage. Who needed rays of sunshine, anyway?

Tiffany stomped forward — right into a blast of wind that almost knocked her off her feet. Thunder rumbled again, louder, closer. The temperature had dropped. Hers wasn't the only storm brewing. One was about to break over her head, too. Maybe she should care about that, but right now she didn't.

'I thought I might find you here.' Jack's voice came from several feet behind her. 'You've been gone for over an hour, Tiff, and the storm is about to hit. Don't you think it's time you came back?'

She turned around to shout, yell, pour out her fury and rage and upset.

Instead she said, with a wobble in her voice that she couldn't control, 'You were gone for months and months. You've only just decided it was time to come back, and look how well that's gone so far. You didn't have to come after me now. I can make it back under my own steam, when I'm ready.'

Since he appeared not to want to let her anywhere near him in any way, emotional or physical, she should be the same way. Except she wanted to grab him and keep him safe somehow, and never, ever let him go.

But Jack didn't leave. Instead, his gaze searched her face. 'You're upset. I wish you hadn't found out, hadn't had to face the worry, but all that — it's over now, Tiff. It's finished with. That's why I came back. So

111

we could go on as before and all that could fall back into the past. That's where it belongs now.'

'It's a past you didn't let me share with you. Did *anyone* even know what you were going through all that time?' That was what gave her such agony. He had been so alone.

She searched his face as her aggression crumbled to make way for deeper concern — worry and, yes, affection. Knowledge of Jack's battle only made her care for him all the more, in all ways. Tiffany wasn't sure how to control that, either. If she saw any sign of the same in him . . .

'I'm sure you worked for your firm over there, as you said, but did your employer even know you were working around your treatment and recovery?' Again she tried not to picture him battling alone, and failed. Her heart ached. 'Here I thought you'd looked on it as a holiday. You should have told all of us, Jack. Mum, Dad, me, my brothers. I can understand why you wouldn't tell your parents, but we all would have supported you.'

'I didn't need anyone to know. I had the best doctors, the best treatment. When I got my strength back fully I came to you.' His hands fisted. He pushed them into the pockets of his jeans.

But even as he pushed her away emotionally, he positioned himself so his broad back bore the brunt of the wind that swirled around them in angry gusts. The eyes that searched her face were concerned and caring, *for her sake,* and sharpened with just a hint of that same something that dwelt inside her. The tiniest hint, but it was there, and Tiffany's heart leapt in response.

She forced herself to remain very still, but she couldn't face silence. 'You never needed to make this a secret, Jack. If you'd told me you didn't want to be involved with me in any other way I still would have been there as your friend. You made it impossible for me to do that.'

As she said those words she forced herself to admit the truth. She still cared for Jack. *In that way.* Even though she had tried to stifle the feelings, they weren't about to be stifled. It was part of the reason all this hurt so much. But she *would* have been a friend to him. Whatever he needed.

Rain started to fall, turned into a deluge and soaked them. Jack stared at her through the sheets of rain, and she stared back, and that certain something in his eyes became far more than a hint — whether he wanted to let it or not.

He took a step towards her, and stopped.

His jaw clenched as his gaze roved over her and came back to her face. Need and awareness, confusion and frustration were all there. And in her, too.

She reached out her hand. 'Jack —'

'We have to get out of this storm.' He muttered the words, grasped her arm, and rushed her towards his Jeep.

Her arm tingled beneath his touch. As they climbed into the Jeep she glanced at him just once, and shivered with something quite different from cold.

Jack stared at her, locked his hands around the steering wheel. If hers hadn't been shaking so much she might have wanted to lift her camera from where it hung around her neck to see if she could capture that expression. But, no. She captured it inside her somewhere, instead. And then Jack put the Jeep in motion and it seemed she held her breath the whole way back.

'Get changed into something dry.' Jack growled the words at Tiffany as they stepped into the cottage. He grabbed a towel from the linen press to dry off, too, strode into his room and shut the door.

Something had happened out there when the rain had begun to fall. He had expected her to still be angry, had been braced for that. He hadn't been ready for compassion and sweet affection that could so easily lead to other things. Then she'd got soaked to the skin, and his body had become blatantly aware instead of simply a little interested.

Well, she would be dry and dressed now, and hopefully he would find some way to defuse that spark of tension they had somehow struck between them.

He left his room dressed in dry clothes and determined to control his thoughts.

Tiffany stood in the kitchen in soft knit pants, bare feet, and a T-shirt that clung to every curve. Her hair sprang out in damp curls all around her head and spilled down over her shoulders. She looked lost and uncertain, and when their gazes met and held she held her breath, and the irises of her eyes disappeared behind pools of black as her pupils dilated.

That was it. Jack just . . . stepped into her expression, and the controlled, conscious, focused and determined version of him disappeared.

What remained stared at her with all the pent-up need and heat that swarmed through him.

'Um, the rain is heavy. It's quite a storm.' Tiffany uttered the banal comment and didn't seem to know where to look. Other than at him. In a way that heated him even more.

Did she know she was doing it?

'A little water never hurt anyone.' He tried for a casual tone. What emerged was more like a dark promise. 'At least the goats have their shelter sheds.'

He had to get out of here. Go back into the rain. Invent some reason to be outside, away from here, away from temptation. His gaze travelled from her damp hair to her feet and slowly back up again. His feet didn't move.

With shaking hands she picked up a teatowel and used it to dry her camera. She bent to set both down very carefully on the bench. She had a sweet butt, soft and shapely, and just right for a man's hands, and it was outlined in glorious detail beneath the soft pants that cupped her from waist to thigh to calves and ankles.

Jack suppressed a groan.

Tiffany stepped forward, away from the sink, gestured vaguely, 'Well, um, I should —'

'I should probably —' Intent on getting out of the way of temptation he steppe.' forward, too.

She zigged. He zagged. They stepped right into each other.

With her body pressed close, the contact he had craved within his reach no matter that he had tried to avoid it, Jack lost the thread that had held his control together.

His arms locked around her.

Hers were as tight about him.

With a soft groan of defeat he dipped his head as she raised hers, and their mouths met and clung.

She tasted of rain and of Tiffany, sweet and special, and all he had dreamed of when he shouldn't have allowed himself to dream at all.

Jack's hand came to rest on the crown of her hair, swept down her back and pressed between her shoulderblades to tuck her even closer against him as he took that taste into his mouth and held it.

Life, reality, truth, meaning — all stopped. Sensation bombarded him from all directions. Her warm body through the simple clothes, the scent of the storm in the air and on her skin, the sounds of it outside the cottage. Sheet after sheet of relentless rain, and the relentless tide inside him of hunger and curiosity and imperative need.

'Tiff.'

'I'm so angry at you, Jack.' One fist closed and thumped against his shoulder, but it was a half-hearted effort. She pressed more into their kiss, desperately and fully.

'This can't happen,' he warned her, and deepened the kiss. He wanted reconciliation with her, and other things. He didn't know the entirety of what he wanted, and he couldn't stop anyway. Because the *only thing he wanted that mattered was this.*

Reasoning fell away. It simply couldn't stand in the face of this. Jack had waited too long, wanted her too much, and his lofty ideals and determination crashed around them and he didn't even hear them fall.

Tiffany pressed up into his hold. He cupped her face, splayed his fingers across her jaw and stroked the tender skin behind her ear. His other arm locked her against him, body pressed to body from neck to knee.

He had needed her, missed her, for so long, and she was warmth and welcome and home in a way he could never feel anywhere else, with anyone else.

Jack forgot his concerns about being like his father, about protecting her, forgot his struggles. He forgot it all in the taste and touch of her. A low sound escaped his throat. The pressure inside him built further, beckoned to him, insisted he find relief in her taste and her touch and her hold.

He lifted his head, told himself he still had

control of this. But he didn't. All the years of loving her, growing up with her, sharing and caring and being close, all the slow build to wanting more than the friendship she'd given so freely tangled together in a need that swamped him. He could only think with that need, and her response to him.

Tiffany watched Jack's face, saw his conflict, and watched him edge towards giving in to his need. Without saying a word, she urged him on.

Kiss me again, Jack. Let us be this way so the barriers are gone between us and I can prove to you that I've a place in your life — not only as your friend, but as more.

She was furious with him — upset, frightened, devastated — and she was enticed by him in equal measure. Yes, she wanted him to trust her, to let her in. Were those emotional needs, or physical ones, or both? Tiffany wasn't even sure any more, but she knew she couldn't stop this. Not when everything inside her said to reach for all this moment could be.

Jack did want. She could see that plainly, and her heart allowed a whisper of hope that somehow overrode even her deep hurt and fear that maybe *this* could bring them together against the odds, against Jack's barriers. Maybe somehow they could break through those things.

'Your hair is going crazy.' It was a tribute, not a judgement, and his gaze travelled with deliberate interest over the wild, tumbling mass.

'I'm going crazy right along with it.' She admitted it, and his gaze darkened more, his mouth softening while a flush of longing coloured his cheeks.

'I can't leave you alone.' The words were wrenched from him. 'I just want to hold you. It shouldn't hurt anything. We were friends, I missed you . . .'

He wasn't just holding her, and they both knew it, but she stayed silent and let his actions speak. One strong arm wrapped behind her back, fingers splayed at the base of her spine as his other hand held her face, angled it. Her hands found their way around his neck and held on as their lips met and clung once again.

In this moment Jack was different, and she absorbed the taste of him, the texture of his lips against her mouth — all of it — and acknowledged how much *more* this was.

Tiffany invested all her pent-up energy and feeling into their kiss, gave herself over to the moment and to him.

Because this was Jack, *her Jack.* She

wanted this. It felt right. Her heart opened to allow only that knowledge, and the truth of his need for her.

'Jack.' His name fell from her lips, breathless, and he answered her with the whisper of her name in a shaken tone.

His hands swept up her back, cupped her shoulders, tangled in her damp hair.

Somehow her back was against the kitchen wall. Jack's hands cradled her close, as though he couldn't bear to let her go. His body strained towards hers. Their hearts beat against each other through the layers of clothes.

'I want you.' He spoke in a deep growl and closed his eyes, his face a harsh mask of desire as he let his fingers play through her hair. 'You're so beautiful, Tiff.'

Did he really see her that way? His eyes opened slowly to reveal slumberous blue depths, and, yes, she saw that opinion reflected there.

This was what she had wanted, longed for. Now it was in her grasp. Jack had realised, let go of foolish worries and accepted. He must have — mustn't he?

Her breath caught, and her gaze tracked the familiar planes and angles of his face. With her hands, she traced his shoulders, his arms, across his back.

'You're beautiful, too. More than I can begin to tell you. Even though I'm still angry at you.' It was important to remind them both of that. But she pressed her lips to the side of his face, the blade of his nose.

She wanted to kiss every feature, to beg him to live and be well, but most of all she wanted this. Their closeness, what they both felt.

Finally, Jack was being honest with her.

'This shouldn't happen.' Jack repeated it, but he caught her mouth with his again, and soon she forgot his words, hers, all of it, as she lost herself in Jack's embrace.

A tempest swept them up. Somehow they were in his bedroom. Jack drew her shirt up and caressed the bare skin of her midriff.

She wanted to touch him, too. It was all so clear now. Jack had been misguided, confused, hadn't allowed these real true feelings between them. That was the real problem. But now he would realise his mistake, and they could build on what had almost begun before he went away.

Jack had to trust her. *This* was the place to start.

A small part of her warned she was allowing her feelings and the stresses of the day to warp her view of reality, but she pushed that thought away. This was the one thing that felt *right.*

'Tiffany.' Jack buried his face against the side of her neck. He clasped her wrists and drew her hands up beneath the loose-fitting shirt, around to touch his bare back. His grip was firm, demanding. The expression in his eyes one of utter absorption. He shuddered, pressed against her, seemed lost in this. So lost.

But they were finding each other. At last they were doing that. This was right, good, exactly what they needed. With this barrier down they could address the other issues. She could make Jack understand how he had wronged her, but that it would be all right now. They would be all right together.

He wasn't going to die. She gave herself the assurance and her arms tightened even more where they held him. Jack was not going to die. He was going to live, and overcome his concerns about them. Already he was moving past those concerns.

Jack lifted her T-shirt over her head. Let it whisper to the floor. His fingers grazed her soft flesh and utter focus filled his face. On this moment, on their togetherness.

He's not really aware of what he's doing. He's not thinking. If he was, he would stop this.

The warning was stronger this time. She

123

still didn't want to hear it.

'I don't want anything to keep us apart.'

Fierce words uttered against the uncertainty that expanded inside her. She tugged at the buttons at the base of his shirt. She wanted her hands on him for real, on every part of him she could reach. Her actions were too close to desperate, but she had to hold onto this focus . . .

Jack had moved in a fog that thickened and sucked him into a swirling mass of feeling and awareness and the hungry, desperate need to connect — to be and to live everything he had denied himself. Tiffany's learning all the truth had somehow released this inside him.

But even the fog couldn't completely shroud his reason, his sense, and gradually Tiffany's desperation made him aware of his own.

What was he doing? It took all of his willpower, but he finally clamped his hand over Tiffany's, stopped her before she could undo any more buttons. How had they reached this point? He shouldn't have allowed it even to start!

If this went on Tiff would want him wholly, and expect the same in return from him. A complete commitment not only to this moment but to her, to them, to what she would want them to be.

His secrets might now be out, and he wasn't happy about that, but still he couldn't give her those things. Instead he would use her, would let this happen when it couldn't ever happen again. All his determination to protect her, to help her keep her distance and get on with her life without the weight of caring for him in this way, would be for nothing.

Jack froze in place — froze somewhere deep down, too, as the reality of his actions bombarded him. This couldn't happen, *period.*

'We have to stop this.' Three buttons hung undone on his shirt. In moments she would have confronted the ugly truth of his wounds.

A sick feeling of panic and despair swept through him. It had nothing to do with the scars he bore.

No. It was because Tiffany was not the kind to give in to passion and then walk away. She deserved better, and better wasn't his to give her because he was too like Samuel. Jack ignored the whisper that said he didn't want her to know the reality of his changed body. That wasn't the point.

'I should never have let this happen.' The

words were wrenched from him even as his body protested the truth of them. He bent his head and moved away from her, handed the T-shirt to her and didn't meet her gaze. 'It wasn't right for you, and I let myself get carried away. I'm sorry.'

'You don't understand what's right for me, otherwise you'd realise —' She broke off, replaced the shirt, stepped around him and headed for the door of the room. A different kind of devastation now shaded her face.

He was to blame for that, too, and he flayed himself with the knowledge. 'What I realise is I've hurt you, because I'm stupid and selfish and let this happen when I shouldn't have.'

A part of him wanted to just take her. But he couldn't do that. He wanted her closeness and friendship again, but he couldn't have it like this.

'You want me to accept this is it. You're shutting the door on all we could have shared, even though you wanted that sharing as much as I did.' As she spoke the words her gaze narrowed with tense hurt, and she gave a harsh laugh. 'For a few moments there I actually thought you and I could get past all that's happened, but you don't want that. You don't want *me enough to want that.'*

'That's not the issue. I told you commitment isn't for me. Samuel's legacy —'

Her glance moved to the foot of the bed, to his travel bag, and then moved to his chest, where the shirt covered all the relevant bits. 'Maybe you truly believe what you said about Samuel. Maybe you think that's a big part of why you shut me out of your life.'

'It's the primary reason.' Why wouldn't she believe that? Why did he feel guilty and conflicted for saying it?

'Well, I think you're wrong about it, and I think there are other reasons that go far deeper, that you aren't acknowledging at all!' She made a frustrated gesture with one hand. 'You're not facing all that's happened to you, Jack. A part of you is holding back from that, and somehow *that's* got to do with you backing away just now. I'm certain of it.'

'You're wrong.' A flat statement with no room for manoeuvring, or consideration, or anything else. 'All that matters to me is you. Your future, your happiness. And that happiness is the reason this had to stop.' Jack shook his head. 'There's been unresolved sexual tension between us. Maybe both of us wondered what would happen if we set it loose. Maybe we just both gave in to stress and curiosity, to being close together after everything was revealed in the sudden way it came about.'

A still silence surrounded them. The rain had ceased, at least for the moment, but it continued unabated inside her. 'It was when I was about to touch your scarring that you came back to your senses and decided to stop things.' Couldn't he see some association there?

'Because we can't go there.' An angry growl rose from his throat. 'Friendship is what we *can* have. It's what I came here to get, and it's what I intend for us. Nothing else. I'm not hung up on my experiences.' His jaw jutted forward. 'I understand how it can impact on survivors, and I've taken care not to let myself feel that way about it.'

'Have you?' She took a step towards him. Let him see the challenge in her expression, her stance. 'Take off your shirt. Let me see this scar that doesn't bother you so much!'

His mouth firmed into a flat line. Any warmth in his eyes disappeared. That empty stare cut across hers until he gave one short, harsh sound from the back of his throat. 'This isn't a sideshow, Tiffany.'

She realised then she had gone too far. Way too far. 'I'm sorry.' She raised one hand towards him, but he was all granite and resistance. She let the hand drop back to her side. 'I'm sorry, Jack. I shouldn't have said that. But you need to let yourself heal — on the inside — and I truly don't believe you have done that.'

'If that's true, and I still don't agree, the only thing that will help me is for you to let our friendship flourish. Help me to enjoy that with you.' His gaze was steady and calm on hers. 'We're back to that, Tiff, and I need you to agree that's what we need to do.'

How could she be a friend to him and nothing else when her body and her emotions cried out for so much more?

Yet if she didn't try, didn't that make her selfish? Didn't it mean she refused to listen to what he wanted? To let him make his choices and live by them? She had told him she deserved the choice. He did, too, even if she didn't like those choices.

'I'll try, Jack.' She would try to be a friend and nothing more, and hope somehow that was possible after all that had occurred between them.

CHAPTER SEVEN

'At least the painter has finished his work, and the walls are dry enough for the furniture to be replaced.' Tiffany muttered the words and told herself to take pleasure in the ordinary, the simple, just as Jack had asked her to do in relation to their friendship when they had discussed the matter two days ago.

They had both tried hard since then — so hard that for her, at least, it was painful. But they *were* trying, and slowly Jack was relaxing with her again. Maybe, over time, he would relax enough to begin to address his concerns about his father, and the deeper issues of his cancer.

For his sake she hoped he would do both those things because she was convinced he hadn't. Not fully. Not enough to allow him to go forward with his life properly. And even if he never wanted her, she still wanted him to have that opportunity.

Even if the thought of him with someone else in that way caused her more pain that she wanted to acknowledge. She had to keep her focus now. Look for ways to encourage Jack to heal. But how? That was the problem. Besides being his friend, she didn't know how to help him.

'Are you there, Tiff?' Jack called the question as he stepped into the farmhouse kitchen.

'Yes. I'm here.' She moved into the room to meet him. 'The painter just gathered the last of his things. Did you see him leave?'

'He stopped to tell me there's more rain on the way.' Jack shrugged. 'I'd just finished work on the shelter shed that developed the leaky roof during the last lot of rain. I thought I'd come back and help you replace the furniture, in case you got any ideas about moving it all yourself.'

'You know me too well.' She offered a smile, and said in self-defence, 'Most of it's not too heavy, and I thought I could push stuff rather than try to lift it.'

'Uh-huh. And it will all be easier to move if there are two of us to do the work.' He smiled back, and that was a start, wasn't it? This mellowing between them, this effort to truly embrace the friendship he wanted and admitted he needed? At least he needed

131

that. Couldn't they go from there?

And what happens when he leaves? The days are ticking away. What if he goes back to Sydney and you lose all the ground you've gained?

Well, she wouldn't let that happen! She would insist they kept in contact this time — would be there for him whether he made it easy for her or not. She would help him and she would deserve his friendship, damn it. If she tried hard enough, she could make it work.

Her birth mother might have rejected her efforts all those years ago, but this was different. And she wasn't hung up about that, either. The focus needed to be on Jack. On his issues, his needs. Not on her paltry history that had no bearing on the here and now.

How is that denial different from Jack's attitude, to his unwillingness to face his demons and deal with them?

It was different because she *had* no issues!

Jack stepped into her parents' living room and bent to lift one of the large armchairs. She watched his muscles flex, and quickly forced her gaze away. That, of course, was the other problem. Her thoughts should be focused on nurturing a relaxed state between them. Not on the idea of Jack flexing his muscles while he moved furniture, or anything else blatantly physical about him.

But how could she forget when he had held her and almost made love to her?

'The man shouldn't be so to-die-for appealing. It doesn't help.' She muttered the words beneath her breath and stomped over to his side, then said more loudly, 'I thought you said we should do this together?'

Jack conceded the point with a dip of his chin, and they set to work moving the rest of the stuff in the room. When they'd finished, he let his glance rove the results. 'It looks good. Do your parents know this is being done?'

'Nope. We decided to surprise them. It was Jed's idea, initially, and we all agreed to chip in to pay for the work.' It was a way for all of them to thank Colin and Sylvia for their devotion to raising them. 'I'm going to ask my brothers about doing the same with the fencing. Mum and Dad aren't broke, but they've invested a lot of money into all of us over the years, and certain aspects of the farm have suffered as a result.'

'Not the dairy, though. It's state of the art.'

'No. They would never scrimp with the goats. But I guess the fencing was something that could be let slide until it started to cause problems. That time seems to be now.'

'Some of it *is* old.' Jack nodded and they moved on to replace the furniture in the rest of the house.

When it was all done, he turned to her. 'How about dinner in town tonight, to celebrate all our hard work?'

'That would be nice.' Her skin prickled, but she did her best to ignore that reaction and think, instead, of ways an evening out might help her to help Jack. That was what she needed to focus on — helping Jack as his good friend, just like old times.

Yes, sure, and nothing at all has changed to make that even the slightest bit difficult to achieve.

'We'll have to shower and change.' The words emerged before she'd thought them through, and her face warmed. 'I mean —'

'I know what you mean.' A tinge of colour rose in his cheeks.

It would be so much easier if he seemed completely uninterested in her, but that wasn't the case. And the ongoing awareness on both sides only made trying to give him what he wanted more difficult. It made her *hope.* Hope that he might change his mind and seek more than just friendship with her after all. That there might be a way forward for that, even though in reality it was clear there was not. The man had more road-blocks up than a flooded country road marked with multiple detours.

They walked back to her cottage in silence. It did indeed look as though another storm was on its way. She thought about that as she chose what to wear, but mostly she thought about her concerns, and about Jack. About the past, the future, uncertainty, trust, fear and . . . hope. Always, despite everything, there was the hope that could hurt her so much.

Then she cleaned up the kitchen and thought about nothing — until Jack stepped back into said kitchen with his hair damp against his head. He smelled wonderful, and she simply couldn't disengage her feelings about him that spoke to the deepest heart of her somehow.

His gaze roved the small room before it came to rest on her, where she stood with her hands immersed in sudsy water at the sink.

'I thought I'd better clean up in here before we left.' She blurted the unnecessary explanation. 'There's nothing worse than coming home to dirty dishes.'

Actually, there were lots of things. She clamped her lips together before anything else silly could come out.

His gaze tracked over her and moved quickly away. Had she imagined it, or had his examination lingered on her butt?

Jack cleared his throat. He moved to stand beside her at the sink, plucked a teatowel from the nearby rail. 'I'll help you finish the dishes before we go.'

'You don't have to —' She swung her gaze towards him, to the broad presence of his shoulders at her side, the firm line of his lips and the examination of sharp blue eyes as they searched her face.

He lifted the dishes up one by one, dried them, and set them on the bench. She kept washing, and asked herself why he wouldn't acknowledge this, or give them a chance.

A smarter question would be why was she wishing for the moon when it was quite clear Jack didn't even want a chunk of space debris? Maybe she needed to stop watching sci-fi reruns on TV, too!

Be his friend. If he says that's what he needs most, then give him that.

'Um, this is the last dish.' She shoved the plate into his hands and quickly drained the water from the sink. 'It was only our lunch things. I should probably clean them all up as I go along each time, but sometimes I'm too busy.'

He took care of the plate and tossed the

teatowel onto the bench. One hand came to rest on his hip. 'Are you ready to go?'

'Nope. I still need lipstick.' This might be a far cry from a date, but she wanted to look half-decent. She offered a small smile. 'Don't worry. I won't take long.'

She stepped into her room and dashed the lipstick over her mouth, then put it in a bright purple mirrored case and dropped that into her handbag. The phone rang just as she emerged with the bag slung over her shoulder.

After a quick glance towards Jack, she stepped into the lounge room and grabbed up the receiver. 'Hello, this is Tiffany.'

'Hello, dear, it's Mum.'

'Hi, Mum. How's the trip going? Everything is good here.' She relayed the cheese production figures, the health of the goats, and minimised any difficulties there had been — all things that would convince Sylvia she was doing a good job. Or rather, *assure* Mum of it. There was no need to convince her, after all.

As Tiffany dealt with the phone call, Jack waited silently in the kitchen, his gaze fixed away from her as he looked out of the window. His shoulders had tensed when the phone rang. They'd relaxed a little now. Maybe he'd wondered if the caller would be

Samuel again.

Tiffany realised she was staring at said shoulders, and made herself stop. Instead, she perched on the end of the sofa and focused her attention fully on her mother.

Well, almost fully. Jack did have beautiful shoulders.

'You're in London today, aren't you, Mum?'

Talk about this wonderful trip you're having, Mum, so I don't think about Jack and broad backs, or anything else along those lines.

'Yes, we're in London.' Her mother discussed a few highlights, and paused to draw a breath. 'You truly are okay without Ron?'

'Things are fine, Mum.' She tried to sound enthusiastic, in control. Indeed, she *was* those things when it came to the business aspects of managing all this. 'Jack and I made time to visit Ron yesterday. He's doing well, and everything on the farm is under control.'

Everything except her personal life. Perhaps she could wave a magic wand . . .

'That's good. I'm relieved to hear it, dear.' Sylvia blew out a breath. The line crackled, and she hurried to wrap up the call. 'It's just a bit scary when your father and I are so far away. We'd hate for you to be under too much pressure or anything, and you and

138

Jack hadn't seen each other for such a long time. I wasn't sure —'

'I'm not under too much pressure. Truly.' And she sure as heck didn't want to talk about Jack.

Tiffany loved her Mum and Dad, but she had never admitted any change of feelings to them where Jack was concerned, and saw no reason to bare her soul now that things were so much more complicated even than before.

Not that she would when Jack stood within hearing distance anyway.

'All right.' Her mother made a soft sound over the line. 'Look after yourself. Dad and I look forward to seeing you when we get home. I'll call again when I can manage, but it might not be too often, depending on how busy the days are.'

Tiffany's hand relaxed around the phone. 'You're welcome to call any time, Mum, but only if you *have* time. Remember I have the itinerary for your trip, with all the hotels listed. If there are any problems I'll let you know straight away. I know phone calls home are expensive.'

'That's quite true.' Sylvia said a quick farewell, passed on Colin's love, and ended the call.

'Sylvia isn't worrying, surely?' Jack came

to her side. His voice softened and he touched her arm, then quickly dropped his hand away. 'You're doing just fine.'

'With your help.' She had to admit that much. 'I think the news about Ron has worried her. Maybe I should have called and told her about it myself.'

'You couldn't have known Denise would tell them.' Jack's gaze tracked over her mouth for a moment, before he lifted his head and strode quickly towards the door.

'Nice shade of lipstick,' he muttered. 'Let's go.'

'I should have guessed about Denise. She likes to talk. Have you got a venue in mind for our dinner?' She followed him out through the door and drew it closed behind her, suddenly overly conscious of the coral-pink gloss on her lips, and of her lips themselves.

Suddenly conscious of herself and Jack in all the ways he didn't want her to be, and didn't want to be himself.

'I hope the food here is okay.' Jack had thought a meal out as friends might help to bring the tension between him and Tiffany into better balance. He should have his awareness of her under control — he *needed* it to be under control — but getting it there was another matter.

Even when he felt annoyed at her for claiming he was avoiding real issues with his concerns about Samuel, and the way he had faced and handled his health issues.

She was wrong, of course, on both counts, and over time she would have to accept that. Just as over time he would stop thinking of her in terms of the way they had come together after getting caught in the rain. Even if his body seemed to want to do nothing but remember the episode.

Well, the trip in the close confines of the Jeep was over now. They could get on with the *friends, dinner, surrounded by people, bland and non-threatening* part of the evening.

He helped her out of the Jeep. Not because this was a date. It wasn't. He did it out of basic courtesy. Surely he could display some simple manners during the evening without it being a problem?

If his fingers tightened around her waist it was because he didn't want to drop her, nothing else.

If his breath stopped in his throat, what of it? Everyone forgot to breathe occasionally.

Yes, but did they ache to be close, to inhale her scent and touch the softness of her skin . . . ?

Enough!

'I'm sure the food will be fine.' Tiffany ran her hands down her thighs and her chin came up. 'From the number of cars and utility vehicles parked outside, the place appears to be hopping.'

His gaze followed the movement of her hands, but he forced that gaze away before it could find its way to her bottom, which was clad in yet another pair of delicious jeans.

They would enjoy this time together and go back to the farm with their friendship cemented a little further. That was *all* this was about. Tonight, and all his time here. He came to her with a goal and he would make that goal work, despite everything.

The doors of the old-fashioned place opened. Country music wafted outward as a man and woman in akubra hats, checked shirts and pointy-toed riding boots stepped outside. The music came from guitars and fiddles, with a strong beat and a lot of energy in it.

See? Not exactly romantic so far. He stretched a smile across his lips. 'Let's go in.'

The music was louder inside. It came from a live band that played at the end of a large dance area beyond the booth seating.

Two thirds of the booths were occupied, and most of the people sported jeans and western wear. A few couples danced to the music. They found a table and took a few minutes to study the menu.

'Are you ready to order?' A middle-aged woman paused beside their table, notepad and pencil stub in hand.

They placed their orders and talked in a desultory way until their meals arrived. Desultory was good.

Jack tucked into chargrilled steak with a baked potato and green beans. Tiffany had chicken Caesar salad. Things were going quite well until they started on the herb loaf. Because they had to eat it *together*, didn't they?

That meant hands reaching at the same time, brushing, and crackles of electricity up his arms and all through his body while she stared at him with luminous eyes that tried so hard not to express anything but friendship.

Let's go out to dinner to get away from it all. Yeah, right.

'How's your meal?' He suppressed his growl and instead gestured towards the food on her plate.

She speared a piece of bacon with her fork. 'It's nice. The Caesar dressing tastes exactly right. Tangy, spicy . . .' Her gaze dropped to his mouth and she trailed off, and then she quickly looked away. 'How is your meal?'

'The steak is good. Well-cooked, tender.' Even these mundane words seemed to hold a hidden meaning that shouldn't be there.

As they finished their meals, the leader of the band that provided the music gave a call for everyone to get on the floor. 'We've got some boot scootin' to do tonight, so come on out here and let's give it a go.'

The western clothes and style of music clicked into place then. These people were into line dancing — an unromantic dance where people didn't even touch or face each other, right?

'Let's join in.' Jack made the decision, and instantly acted on it. They would have people, total strangers, all around them, and he could burn off some surplus energy at the same time. It was the first smart idea he'd had all night. Maybe he could even salvage the evening. 'C'mon, Tiff.'

They might never before have done anything that involved akubra hats and pointy boots and an enthusiastic if less than perfect rendition of a song about blue heeler dogs and dusty Outback roads. But if they danced, they wouldn't be close — would simply be part of a big group of people.

'Wouldn't you like to be in the line dance with the others?'

'Yes.' She got to her feet immediately. 'It'll be a nice . . . distraction.' As she spoke those words, warm colour rose in her cheeks.

His pulse-rate lifted simply because she'd confirmed, even if she hadn't meant to, that she was as aware of him as he was of her.

Jack tried to ignore that reaction, got to his feet, and led her over to join the line-up. Fun. They'd have some innocent fun — cool things off a bit before they left.

What followed *was* fun. It was also friendly, noisy and loud as they endeavoured to learn the dance moves. The dancers were welcoming, and the band's lead singer called out encouragement throughout each song.

After several numbers, the singer suggested they were all almost ready for the annual Tamworth line dance and country music festival. From the crowd's response, many of them made it a point to go each year.

'They want to be in the biggest line dance in the world.' Tiffany whispered the words into his ear in the short break before the band struck up again.

Jack tried to suppress his body's response

to that simple act. 'Did Tamworth actually make it into the record books for the biggest line dance?'

'I'm not sure whether they made it or not.' She murmured it, and a new set started, and away they went again.

Later, somewhat breathless and a little dishevelled, they paused once again as the music stopped. Jack was about to suggest they sit down, have one long, cool, stay-away-from-each-other drink and then head home. It was a good, sound, rational intention. At the least it was better than his idea of this night out in the first place.

But the band called an end to the line dancing for the night, and the leader pinpointed *them,* thanked them for joining in the fun, and asked them to lead off the couples dancing.

Refusal wouldn't exactly have been polite, so Jack drew Tiffany into the most relaxed embrace he could, and they started to dance. In moments the floor was full, and they were enclosed in their own world in the middle of all those moving couples.

In the centre of that crowd, with Tiffany in his arms but not truly his to hold, loneliness struck Jack, clawed at him from the inside out. Heartache. Broken dreams.

He had fought it, ignored it, told himself

he didn't care about it, but tonight it had somehow managed to break free of the hold he always kept over it to bombard him at the worst possible moment.

He could not have the life with Tiffany that he had dreamed of, hoped for, before everything went belly-up.

The pain of that truth struck hard and suddenly, as he acknowledged maybe he *had* pushed certain things away rather than really facing them.

He hadn't meant to, but somehow it had happened. And Tiff was the one he wanted. The only one. The kisses they had shared were amazing, but he wanted her even more deeply than that. He didn't even want to consider how deeply those needs might be entrenched in him.

Coming here, seeking out her friendship again, had been naïve, and now it was too late. He knew it. What was he going to do?

Against his volition, his hand urged her forward, until their bodies pressed together and he could bury his face in the crown of her hair. If she had resisted maybe he would have held back, but she didn't.

After a moment's hesitation she wrapped her hand around the side of his neck. The other gripped his upper arm, and she sighed as though in acceptance — or perhaps confusion. Maybe both.

Jack got that. He felt the same way, yet he couldn't let her go. His arms just wouldn't do it.

Instead, he tucked her in even closer as they swayed to the music, and he told himself this would be fine. They had an audience, chaperones, and when the dance ended *this would end,* and that would be that.

Jack drifted until the music stopped. Then he tried to pull himself back together. He released Tiffany and stepped back. 'We should go.'

The tone of his voice said he didn't want to.

But she nodded and stepped back, too. 'Of course.'

When they emerged from the building, she drew a deep breath and looked up at the sky. 'I think the painter's weather prediction was right. There's rain on the way.'

And rain inside him. Jack missed her closeness already, missed holding her. How would he walk away at the end of his time here? Had it been a mistake to come at all?

Jack suppressed a frustrated sigh and helped her into the Jeep, then climbed in and started the journey home.

Or rather, to Tiffany's cottage. It wasn't

his home and never would be, and he needed to remember that.

As the kilometres ticked by his tension rose rather than fell. She was silent, and he sensed she held herself in check.

Maybe you could be different. Maybe you could overcome your similarity to Samuel and be with her that way.

But there was more to it than simply that. Even if Samuel's influence was no longer an issue, Jack couldn't let her buy into his life and the uncertainty ahead of him.

He had years of ground to cover before he would be declared truly free of the cancer that had attacked his body. And even then no iron-clad guarantee that it would never come back. He didn't intend to live in fear, and he planned to have a very long life, but he couldn't offer that certainty to anyone, and Tiffany deserved more than to worry about such things.

Fifty eight minutes after they'd set out, Jack turned the Jeep in at the farm's gateway. Every one of those minutes had made themselves felt both in the painful process of his thoughts, and in his knowledge of her nearness.

And now he didn't know how to end the evening easily.

'Shouldn't we get out? We're here.' Her

words held a whisper of the same things he struggled with right now.

And that undermined him.

Get out of the Jeep. Say goodnight and forget this night ever happened.

'Wait there.' The wind ripped against her door when he opened it. He pushed it wide and stood in the gap so it couldn't slam shut on her. 'Out you get.'

She stepped down, but he got the timing wrong and didn't step away as quickly as he should have. Instead of her feet hitting the ground, she bumped into him. He awkwardly grabbed her, her hands clutched onto his shoulders, and that easily she was in his arms again.

Hazel eyes swirled with confusion, and with the same temptation he felt.

Jack let go of her and backed away. 'Go inside. Go into your room now, and shut the door.' The words warned her, but most of all they warned him.

'Why? Because you don't want me?' She drew back far enough to stare into his eyes. 'You know, your actions may not match your words, but I've got the message, Jack. No matter how tempting, you won't willingly accept any feelings towards me that aren't platonic. Not while you're in control of your thoughts, anyway. I guess our dance together tonight snuck up on you.'

'Don't push me, Tiffany. Not tonight.' When Tiffany would have rushed past him, Jack caught her hand in his. His fist curled around her soft fingers. 'Just . . . don't push, okay?'

'Then stop seeing me the way you do. Because I see you that way, too, and I can't fight it when I know you feel the same things.' The words burst from her, broken, emotional, hurting. 'And I hurt for what you've been through, and how you shut me out.'

'I'm not shutting you out.' He wrapped her against his chest. Right there against the side of the Jeep, with the cottage behind them and the hum of the oncoming storm in the night air, Jack wrapped her close, offered silent comfort, and drew comfort from her nearness. 'I'm not shutting you out as my friend, Tiff. I don't ever want to do that.'

'I'm afraid you will. I'm afraid we'll lose that — lose everything.' She hugged him back, so tightly.

He dipped his head, and she looked up. Their noses bumped. That was all, but it was so much more, and Jack realised if he didn't do something this would end in her bed, with him buried inside her, whether it was right or wrong. And then they *would* lose everything.

No matter what thoughts he might have had, what ways he might have looked for to ignore what was right for her, he couldn't ignore those things.

So he made a hard decision and hoped she would understand. 'I don't want to have to leave, Tiff. Not until my time is up here. And then I want to be able to come back, to see you often, to just be with you.'

He forced himself to let go of her and step back. 'I'm going to sleep at your parents' house for the remaining few days. Now that the furniture is back in place, there's no reason why I shouldn't. It will be better that way.'

When she didn't speak, he hesitated for a moment, then strode into the cottage. When he stepped outside again, with his travel bag in his hand, she straightened away from his Jeep.

She didn't yell or snap or snarl. Instead she looked at him with utter composure. 'I'll support your choice to sleep at Mum and Dad's house. I'll support all your efforts to maintain our friendship, because I don't want to lose it, either.'

That was good. Really good. His hand tightened on the grip of his travel bag. 'I'm glad you understand —'

'Actually, I think I understand better than you do.'

Tiffany tossed those words at Jack, dropped them into the air with all the control she could muster. Because she wasn't controlled, she wasn't calm, and she could no longer bite back what she wanted to say.

'Do you really know what you want any more, Jack? Because I'm not sure I know.'

His kiss the other night had touched parts of her she had tried so hard to protect — parts that had been hurt once by him. He had the capacity to hurt her even more, and he was doing it now by withdrawing. Even if he believed it was for all the right reasons.

'I didn't intend to push you.' She truly hadn't, but with his determination to draw so far back from her, what choice did she have but to address this? Did she have anything more to lose? 'But I have to ask this, Jack. Can you look me in the eyes and tell me you're facing your life honestly? All of it? The bits to do with the cancer, and with Samuel, and with . . . me?'

When he would have spoken, she went on.

'Because my attempts to do that aren't working out very well right now.' Oh, that was an understatement. 'Before you went away I thought I wanted something special

153

with you, something even more than what we had. Now I just think about surviving the next day, and the next and the next, while I try to work out how to fix the impossible. How to make you see everything you need to see without pushing for what I want for myself. Do you understand, Jack? Do you understand what I'm saying? I want to help you, and I don't know how to do that.'

'This is about *you,* Tiff. It's always been about you.' The words were drawn from him, low and frustrated, but steady, far too steady. 'I thought friendship would be okay. It has to be okay. Otherwise there's nothing.'

For the first time emotion throbbed in his voice. 'My life has too many shadows. I'm sorry I gave in to something I couldn't follow through with on the day of the storm. I shouldn't have. I've got baggage, Tiff. The sort that would drag you down with me. If I can't control myself in close quarters, then I'll take a step further away. But I want you as my friend. I don't want to lose that, too. I've . . . lost too much already.'

Those final words emerged in a tone barely above a whisper. He seemed surprised by them. But finally he was admitting to some of those shadows. Now, if they could talk them through and she could get him to see sense . . .

She swung to face him. 'Your family —'

'Are as dysfunctional and messed-up as it gets, and I'm the result of that gene pool.' Jack tossed his bag into the Jeep and climbed in. 'I'm not fit for an intimate, committed kind of relationship. I regret it, but I'm just not.'

Clearly, to his mind, that was the end — all discussion over and done with. And she had only just tried to begin.

Emotion churned through her and her mouth worked. She couldn't find the right words, if there even *were* any. Why couldn't Jack see reason? He couldn't be right about his family tree.

He just . . . couldn't. And there was so much else he needed to deal with — things that would bring them together. Yes, the two of them. If he truly wanted that. Which brought her back to her earlier observation that he didn't want her enough.

Tiffany's shoulders tried to slump, and she forced them back by her will alone. He *didn't* want her enough. She knew that, had realised that. Tonight had only proved it even more. But she still had a duty to him as his friend to help him through this rough patch in his life — even if he was allowing her in only belatedly, and on his own terms.

The trouble was, she didn't know how to

get through to him. But obviously nothing else was going to happen tonight, so she might as well let him go.

'Goodnight, Jack. Everything you'll need is in the linen closet in the hallway at Mum and Dad's house. There are no perishables in the fridge, so come to the cottage for breakfast, okay?'

With a nod, Jack started the Jeep and drove into the darkness.

And he cursed as he drove the track to Tiffany's parents' house. If he wanted to protect Tiffany, *and he did,* he had to control their relationship a lot better than he had to date. Starting right now.

It had nothing to do with his history, it was just common sense. And the sooner she realised and accepted that, the better.

CHAPTER EIGHT

The phone call came the next morning, just as they'd finished the milk storage. Jack watched Tiffany answer it in the small dairy office. A moment later, she passed the phone to him.

'It's Dr Fennessy from Ruffy's Crossing hospital.' Her tone held puzzlement and concern.

The doctor didn't waste words. Jack's father had been injured in a farm accident. He was in 'a stable condition,' but Jack's presence at the hospital was requested.

Jack's hand tightened around the phone. 'I'm about an hour away, but I'll leave right now.'

'I'm coming with you.' Tiffany tugged off her coveralls and offered a determined look from clear, wide eyes. 'I can wait in the corridor, just be there . . .'

He could waste time arguing, say her presence wasn't necessary, but in truth, her company would be appreciated. Jack nodded, and they cleaned up and hurried to his Jeep.

An hour later they pulled to a stop in the hospital's parking lot and made their way inside to the Admissions desk.

'I'm Jack Reid. Dr Fennessy asked me to come in.'

The busy woman behind the desk rose. Several buzzers rang one after another, and with a frown she quickly joined them and opened a door to the left. 'Please go in. Excuse me.' With that, she was gone again.

The room was an office. A man in his forties rose from behind the desk. 'Mr Reid? Thank you for being so prompt. I'm Dr Fennessy. As I told you when I called, I examined your father when he arrived this morning. I'd like to ask you some questions.'

His glance moved towards Tiffany, dropped to their hands, one large, one smaller, clasped together in a comforting hold.

When had that happened? And how could Jack have not consciously noted it, simply accepted the contact with her? 'This is my friend Tiffany Campbell . . .'

'Perhaps I should wait outside?' They had closed the door, but Tiffany gripped the doorknob with her free hand.

'Actually, Ms Campbell, I would prefer it if you'd stay — unless Mr Reid has any objection?' The doctor studied them both for a moment before he went on. 'You've both been mentioned by Mr Reid senior this morning. As you're here together, a discussion between the three of us might be appropriate.'

'Whatever you think will be helpful.'

'Of course.'

Jack and Tiffany spoke at the same time. Jack turned to offer her a small smile.

'Very well. What I'd like to discuss —' The doctor broke off as the door abruptly opened.

Jack's mother barged into the room. After a brief glance towards Jack and Tiffany, she glared at the doctor. 'Why have you left me ignored in a room with no one to answer my questions? I want to take my husband home.'

With a sweep of her hand, she indicated Jack and Tiffany. 'And what is the meaning of *their* presence?'

'You were asked to wait until I was ready to speak with you, Mrs Reid, but as you've joined us now we might as well *all* get straight down to business.' The doctor gestured towards the chairs in front of his desk. 'Please, will you all be seated?'

While Jack and Tiffany moved towards the chairs, Eileen Reid closed the door and pressed back against it in a resistant pose.

'I tell you, Samuel is fine. He didn't fall very far. He was just stunned for a moment.' She waved a hand. 'I told the farm foreman there was no need to bring him in!'

'Your husband fell from partway up a wheat bin ladder. He has a sprained ankle and a bruised shoulder, and might have had head or internal injuries.' The doctor snapped the words. 'The foreman did the right thing, despite you dismissing him from the hospital the moment you yourself arrived.'

'Well, I was still dressing when the commotion happened —'

'Have you checked for all possible injuries?' Jack rapped out the question, and stopped abruptly. He offered the doctor an apologetic grimace. 'Sorry. I'm sure you have, but . . . is Samuel okay? There's nothing terribly wrong?'

'Your father will recover completely from his *current* injuries.' The doctor's gaze seemed to soften a little.

But his words, although of some comfort, still made Jack's brows draw down. 'Current?'

'I want to take my husband home.' Eileen's face had paled, and her hand trembled as she raised it to her throat. 'Whatever nonsense this is, I insist you release Samuel to me. You've been upsetting him with questions, and you made me leave the room when I pointed that out!'

The doctor's face became a grim mask. 'Your husband will remain in the hospital to undergo a series of tests and evaluations on an old skull fracture and suspected resulting neurological trauma, Mrs Reid. Those questions were important.'

'You don't know what you're talking about.' Eileen looked ready to storm out of the room, but she also looked almost . . . trapped.

Jack was completely confused. 'I'm sorry, Dr Fennessy. I'm afraid I don't understand.'

'When I examined your father today, I was concerned about some of the patterns I saw in his mood and behaviour.' The doctor held up a hand when Jack's mother tried to interrupt him. 'During that examination, I found evidence of a skull fracture that appears to have occurred decades ago. Your father confirmed he once had a horse-riding accident.'

Jack's confusion grew. 'I don't know of any accident of that kind.'

'Your father also informed me the injury

he sustained at that time was your fault.' Although the man's eyes bored into Jack's, Jack could see no accusation there. Just some kind of determination Jack didn't understand. 'In fact, your father seems to believe many of his life's ills are your fault.'

That much Jack got. He swallowed the unexpected shaft of pain, and kept his voice carefully even. 'My father and I don't have a cordial relationship, I'm afraid.'

'In fact, Samuel seems to feel quite a bit of resentment towards you, and some towards your friend here.' The doctor gestured to Tiffany.

Jack tightened his hold on Tiffany's hand. 'Tiffany got on the wrong side of Samuel when we were children. It wasn't her fault.'

He had to be open with the doctor. It could make a difference to the care Samuel received. Jack squared his shoulders, glanced at his mother, and said quietly, 'Family life as a whole hasn't agreed with Samuel, and in particular he feels very angry towards me. It's no surprise to me that he's extended that anger to my friendship with Tiffany. I can only assure you I haven't sought ill-will with my father.'

Eileen had fallen oddly silent, but now she burst into speech. 'Doctor, I *insist* you let me take Samuel home. Whatever he's said about old nonsense is no doubt the result of some confusion . . .'

'Is it, Mrs Reid?' The doctor turned to Jack. 'May I see your driver's licence?'

Eileen frowned. 'Why would you want to see that? What could an old accident matter, anyway?'

Jack certainly didn't know the answers, but he produced his wallet from his jeans pocket and handed over the licence.

The doctor examined it, and handed it back. 'According to the date of birth on your licence, and your father's recollection of the date of his riding accident, you were just months old when the accident occurred. An accident that fractured Samuel's skull, and which I am quite certain is responsible for his rages and a variety of other neurological symptoms, including mood swings, depression and headaches.'

'Are you saying Samuel's behaviour is the result of a head wound?' Jack said the words, but could barely comprehend them. His father's behaviour *wasn't* brought on by his unsuitability to family life? It was too fantastical to believe. Jack addressed the rest of the doctor's words. 'I can't confirm anything about the dates. As I said, I have no recollection of such an accident.'

The doctor cut a glance towards Jack's

mother. 'Interesting, then, that Samuel Reid blames his son for an accident that happened when that son was a mere baby.'

Tiffany's hand rose to close over Jack's arm. 'If this is true . . .'

Eileen shook her head. 'I'm sure I don't know what you mean, Doctor.'

'There *wasn't* a horse-riding accident, witnessed by two farmhands who have since left your employ, one of whom I spoke to by phone this morning, confirming your husband's recollection of events?' The doctor raised his brows. 'It *didn't* happen when your horse shied and pushed into Samuel's mount, making it rear and throw him?'

Anger swept over Eileen's thin features then. As though pushed beyond endurance, she pointed a finger at Jack. 'It was your fault. If you'd been a good baby, I wouldn't have felt so tired and screamed when something fluttered beside the trail. It was just a little fall. But I couldn't let the doctors blame me, and Samuel just needed time to get over it.'

'My God.' Tiffany gasped.

A slow anger began to build inside Jack as his mother's words penetrated. Not rage, but flat, controlled disbelief. 'You let Samuel go through that and didn't get medical care for him? And then you blamed it all on

164

me and made sure he did, too?'

His mother had always been cool, distant — but this?

'You were a bad baby, always crying. And he shouldn't have loved you better. He stopped after that.' She turned her head away.

Did she feel any regret? Any shame at her behaviour? Jack felt his muscles lock. Maybe later this would hurt him. Or maybe he would simply accept that it was nothing more than an extension of the uninterest he had received from Eileen all his life, despite his efforts to reach out to her.

Jack drew a deep, steadying breath, and then he addressed the woman who had given birth to him. 'It's not your fault your horse shied. That was an accident. It could have happened to anyone.' Perhaps if his mother — if *Eileen* realised that, she would understand the rest?

Pity rose inside Jack. Her existence had never shifted beyond the surface of life, beyond her own desires and selfish interests. 'But you should have made sure Samuel received medical care for his injuries, and you shouldn't have encouraged him to hate me.'

Eileen's mouth worked as she seemed to realise she might be in trouble. She turned

165

a pleading look on the doctor. 'It was an accident. It wasn't my fault.'

The doctor stepped past Eileen, opened the door of the room and gestured beyond it. 'The only thing working in your favour at this moment is that the farmhand who saw the incident agrees with you. I'm putting your son in charge of your father's care. I'd like you to return to your farm. You may think yourself lucky if you come out of this with a warning. Much of that will depend on whether your son and your husband choose to pursue this matter further or not.'

He didn't allow Eileen the luxury of deciding to argue or not. At a nod from the doctor, a passing administrative aide stepped to her side, to escort her to her car in the parking lot.

The doctor sighed and closed the door again. 'I hope you can assist me in this, Mr Reid. I want to do those tests and assessments . . .'

'I'll do everything I can to make sure Samuel receives whatever treatment he needs.' Jack made the commitment without hesitation.

Tiffany examined Jack's strong face as he spoke. This must have hurt him so much, yet he was putting his father's needs first, despite all he must be going through and feeling right now.

Her heart ached for him. She wanted to wrap him up in her hold and never let him ever set eyes on Eileen again.

At least Tiffany had been taken from her birth mother and placed into better care. Jack had dealt with Eileen all his life, had tried to give her respect and affection even though Eileen had held herself distant from him. All that time the woman had resented Jack, had begrudged him the few short months of affection he'd apparently received from Samuel right at the beginning.

It was Jack's *mother* who was the real villain here.

'Would you like to visit your father now?' The doctor pushed his hands into the pockets of his coat. 'It might reassure you. After that, I'd like to schedule a second meeting for this afternoon — say, two o'clock? — to speak about what's ahead for Samuel.'

'I'll come to the meeting, and, yes, I want to see him.' A muscle in Jack's jaw worked, and he dropped his gaze before raising it again to meet the doctor's glance. 'But he probably won't want to see me. I don't want to do anything to upset him.'

'Keep your visit brief.' The doctor gave a nod. 'That's all I ask.'

The doctor told them what room to go to and walked away.

'Come with me, Tiff.' Jack hesitated and swallowed. 'If he gets upset, we'll both leave. I just need to see he's okay.'

It was the first time Jack had actively asked her to do anything like this. Heat prickled behind Tiffany's eyes as she nodded. 'Let's go.'

The room was small. It held a bed and a locker, two chairs, and a door that probably led to a small bathroom. Samuel lay in that bed. He seemed smaller somehow. Perhaps it was his pallor, or maybe it was because he looked at Jack with as much confusion as rancour.

Samuel didn't look at Tiffany at all. If that helped keep him calm, it was fine with her. She stood at Jack's shoulder and hoped Samuel would control himself long enough for Jack to assure himself the older man was okay.

'I won't disturb you. I just came to see if you're all right.' Jack stepped closer to the bed and his gaze searched Samuel's face. 'Is there anything you need? Anything you want from the staff here that they aren't doing already?'

'No. There's nothing.' The words were gruff. Samuel's fingers clenched into a fist on top of the covers. But he didn't yell, and he, too, searched Jack's face, as though really looking at it for the first time in a long time. 'The doctor wants to do some tests.'

Jack nodded. 'They might be a good idea. And I thought . . . maybe you might like it if . . . Mum had a holiday before you get out of hospital. I could make the arrangements. Just so you don't have to think about it all right now.'

Samuel thought about rejecting Jack's offer. Tiffany saw the response in his face, expected him to give it voice. But in the end he didn't.

'I want to see my foreman. I don't want the farm falling apart while I'm not there. You can organise your mother's holiday. And then you can go about your business and keep out of mine!' It was a command in a gruff tone, with a fair-sized lashing of the old irritation, and after he gave it he turned his head away.

Tentatively, Jack touched his father's arm, then let his fingers drop away. Then he turned, walked to the door. 'We can have as much or as little to do with each other as you want.'

'Hmph!' The sound wasn't particularly positive.

They left the room. Tiffany hurried to

keep up as Jack strode out of the hospital and across the parking lot, opened the Jeep, and climbed inside.

Jack drew a deep breath then, and turned a rather stunned gaze to her. 'I've got a lot to do. I have to make sure Samuel gets all the help he needs.'

He sat there with his hands gripped around the wheel and stared straight ahead, shook his head once, and again.

'I'm so sorry, Jack.' The words were almost a whisper, but he turned his head and his gaze came into focus on her face.

Tiffany tried to smile for him.

Jack's features softened as he stared at her, and then some of his anger finally hit the surface. Words poured out as he clenched his hands around that wheel. 'How could she do this? Can anyone be that self-absorbed, with never a twinge of guilt?'

'It was very wrong of Eileen, and you were more than kind in return, even in the face of what she did.'

'It was criminal of her to let Samuel's accident pass unremarked and unattended all that time.' Jack thumped one hand against the steering column. 'What if he could have got help? He's been so unhappy, and maybe that didn't need to happen. I could haul her into court and have her punished for what

170

she's done.'

Except Jack would never do that, no matter how angry he was. Instead, he would find some way to make this work for Samuel. He was already on the way to doing that.

Tiffany reached for his hand and curled her fingers around it.

Jack sighed. 'Samuel has turned it all on me over the years because Eileen's convinced him I made him that way. I've resented him so much, Tiff, but *she* was the cold one, the one with no feelings.'

'That's not your fault.'

'I know, but things have been that way for a lot of years.' He released her hand and finally started the Jeep. 'I need to speak to a travel agent. I don't want Eileen around Samuel while the doctors are trying to help him. I don't think I want to see her again for the moment, but I guess I'll have to, briefly, to make it clear this trip isn't optional, and that I expect changes in her outlook when she comes back. I've got the right to demand that much.'

He drew a breath. 'Samuel's foreman is committed to him. I'll ask him to keep his eye on things, keep me informed.'

It took Jack the rest of the day to get things sorted, but sort them he did. Tiffany marvelled at the single-minded dedication he showed as he got to the bottom of all the issues and ensured the right steps were taken to assess and deal with those issues.

His mother was shipped off to a holiday resort. She made a few token protests of concern for her husband — rather belated! — but ultimately Eileen yielded to the temptation of being waited on hand and foot for the next four weeks. Tiffany doubted the woman's nature would undergo any significant turnaround, but, as Jack said, she would be out of the way for a while.

It turned out the foreman had little respect for Eileen. He agreed to take all necessary steps to be of help.

Finally, after several trips between Ruffy's Creek, the Reid farm and the dairy and back again, Jack and Tiffany were able to return to the dairy for the night. Both were emotionally drained. There hadn't been a chance to discuss the impact of all this on their relationship, or even on Jack's outlook towards himself.

'I want to do the chores now — everything that has to be done — even if I'm still out there at midnight.' Jack's voice was hoarse with suppressed strain. 'You go inside, go to bed. Get some rest.'

Leave him to fret about this even more

alone? Not this time, Jack Reid!

'I'm a little restless myself.' Before he could object, she reeled off a list of chores that would keep his hands occupied for hours. And then she helped him do them, and let him soak in all that had happened whilst hope softly built inside her, too. Because this *did* change things. It eliminated the roadblock Jack had claimed to be the biggest.

And if she felt uncertain that he would greet the fact with the same enthusiasm she felt, she refused to allow herself to doubt. It was great news. Jack would admit it was great news when she gently pointed it out, and they would go from there.

When they returned to the cottage it was late. She heated two frozen dinners and they ate them straight out of the packages at the kitchen table.

'Why don't you sleep here tonight? I don't want to think of you over at the house on your own.' She pushed the empty food container away from her, and searched Jack's weary face. 'This has been a tough day for you, Jack.' She drew a deep breath, and drew her courage around her, too. 'But it's not all bad.'

When he didn't respond, she pushed on. 'When you have time to absorb it, I hope you'll be pleased to know you don't have a genetic predisposition towards uncontrolled rages. I'll bet you only got angry at Samuel because he hit some hot buttons of yours.'

'He attacked things that mattered to me, and that I already felt raw and upset about. I can see that now.' Yet Jack didn't sound happy to discover this.

He sounded weary and fed-up and at the end of his rope.

Doubt attacked her. Maybe she should have kept these words to herself until tomorrow, until he'd had time to come to grips with everything else, but she wanted him to have hope — as she now did. Hope that could bring them together in truth.

Was it so wrong to want that when they were both attracted to each other and had . . . feelings for each other? At least of strong affection — or he wouldn't want to hold on to her friendship no matter what, would he?

But Jack got up from the table and stepped away from her. In fact, he didn't stop moving until he reached the kitchen door. 'Tiff, I *have* been thinking. All day.'

The words sounded ominous enough that she got up, too, and braced her body even though she didn't know what was ahead.

Jack did, and he didn't mince his words.

'Today, a lot of things coalesced in my mind. I'm not like Samuel and I never will be. Maybe if he gets some help, one day I'll be able to be around him without him trying to push my buttons and we might manage some kind of relationship. But even if not, I know I won't turn into what he's been.'

'That's a great thing, Jack.'

'Yeah, and I hope something can be done to ease him.' His body seemed to tighten into a hard slab of tension as he went on. 'I think it's most likely he'll go on living with Eileen in their chilly relationship, and I can live with that if it's what he wants, even though I think it's sad.'

Some of that sadness reached her, and with it came a sense of uncertainty, because Jack looked so solemn, and *seemed* so solemn, and something told her this wasn't only about his parents' situation.

'There's no way to put this easily, Tiff, so I'm just going to say it.' He pushed his hands into his pockets. His gaze was steady on hers, too steady, and he went on. 'I've realised our friendship won't make it if we go on the way we have been. I'm too close to you, and I've given in to temptation once already. I thought I could overcome that, but it can't happen again. I need some time and space to refocus on what it is I really want with you.'

She wanted him to want something different, but no words would come out to express that feeling. They were locked inside her, silenced by the flat determination on his face.

'Now that I have things in order for Samuel, I'm going back to Sydney tomorrow. I called Cain late this afternoon, when we came back here so you could check on things in the dairy.' His words dropped like stones at her feet.

She started to shake her head, but he went on.

'I asked your brother to come and replace me in the morning. Later, when some time has passed, we can see each other and spend some time again on our friendship . . .'

His hand gripped the door and he pushed it open. Regret filled his gaze. 'We'll stay close, Tiff. It will just be easier to get the right balance if I go back to Sydney now, give us a breathing space. That's all it is — a breathing space. Then we'll start to see each other again, in sensible increments —'

'Like dishing out measured food portions to a pet so it doesn't act the glutton?' Well, she had reached the end. She couldn't do this any longer. 'I wanted to help you heal.

I'd have done that as your friend.'

'I am healed. Why won't you believe that?' Jack walked out through the door and closed it.

Tiffany glared at that flat plane of painted wood. Damn Jack Reid anyway.

And damn her feelings for him. What could she do now?

Minutes later rain began to lash the cottage on roof and sides, windows and walls. She lay in her bed and stared at the ceiling and really wasn't sure she would even feel it if the house fell in on her.

CHAPTER NINE

It stormed and rained until almost morning. Tiffany knew this because she didn't sleep until an hour before dawn. When she dragged herself out of the cottage into a grey and watery world, her parents were walking towards her from their car.

They had gumboots on, and were dressed ready for work, and for a moment she thought they were a mirage. When she realised they weren't, she wanted to burst into tears.

But Jack was slogging up the track from the house in a pair of her father's gumboots, and she refused to give way in front of him. When he caught sight of her parents he faltered and his head came up. Maybe he was as surprised as she by their arrival. But Jack could now leave with impunity, without even having to wait for Cain to arrive, or get through the milking first, or whatever he had planned to dish out as his idea of fair and equitable.

That should make him happy.

Fine. Good. Tiffany couldn't wait for him to go, either. Let him hold on to all his worries and rob her of the chance to be there for him yet again. Let him bear all the burden about his family without so much as letting her care less about that, too.

Before her thoughts could go any further, Tiffany turned back to face her parents, and forced a smile that could have broken teeth if it was any stiffer. 'You're home early. This is a surprise, but I'm so glad to see you.'

'Good morning, love.' Her mother looked at Jack for a moment, and then pulled Tiffany into a tight embrace. 'The rain has washed a section of fence out between those two paddocks over there. We saw it as we drove in. We're just in time to help out a bit, by the look of things.'

Jack joined them, and greeted her parents. Had he lain awake all night, too? Or was he at peace about walking away from her? Was he dodging truths about himself, or simply putting distance between them because he sensed how much she wanted to break down that distance and in the end, despite their attraction, he didn't want that?

Her father murmured something to Jack, and they walked off together. Tiffany watched them go, and her heart fell apart.

Why deny it any longer? She'd loved Jack as long as she could remember, and now she loved him so utterly she didn't know how she would ever get over it. Those feelings had been there, had grown despite everything, and now they were so big she didn't know how to contain them.

And it was all so hopeless. She turned to Sylvia, intercepted a look that saw too much. 'He's had a lot of difficulties, Mum.' She explained briefly about Samuel, the accident and Eileen. 'He's going now, but it's not because of his mother or father.'

'I guessed as much, dear. We phoned Cain when we got to Sydney Airport. He told us Jack had asked him to come to the farm.'

So Sylvia had also guessed things hadn't worked out between Jack and Tiffany. Well, she should have realised her shrewd mother would read between the lines. 'Cain won't have to come now. I suppose you told him that?'

Without waiting for a response Tiffany started towards the paddock with the damaged fence. 'At least it's an internal fence this time.' Then, fiercely, as her mother kept pace silently beside her, 'Jack should go right now. There's no reason for him to stay now that you and Dad are back.'

180

They didn't speak of it again.

When they'd walked some distance, Tiffany turned to Sylvia with an apologetic glance. She hadn't even asked after them. 'Why the early return? You're both okay? Nothing went wrong?'

'No. We were a little homesick.' Mum pulled a wry face. 'But the trip was a wonderful experience — one we'll treasure. We've got a lot of great memories. It's just that when they started to say bad weather could be on the way, we decided to shift our flight forward and come back in case we got stuck over there.'

Tiffany drew a deep breath. 'Well, the timing is great. It couldn't be better.' She worked hard to make the statement sound casual, ordinary, instead of something that ate at her insides.

Do you know I can't make him want me, Mum? No matter how much I want him? That I can't even get him to share his troubles with me? He almost died but he won't really talk about it. He won't let me in. I'm not enough for him.

Her mother gave her a thoughtful look. 'Let's get the goats in for milking. That's the first step.'

Yes, and then Jack would go. As Tiffany would rather be fully occupied when that happened, she nodded. 'I tried to keep things in good order while you were away.'

'I'm sure you've done a great job.' Sylvia laid a hand on her arm. 'I've always had faith in you, Tiffany.'

Well, Jack didn't have that faith.

The thought came to Tiffany before she could hold it back. She sighed and smiled at her mother. 'Let's get to work.'

After Jack left she could face the hurt inside her.

Later. You can fall apart about it later. First you have to see him off with your head up high.

The four adults fanned out to drive the goats towards the milking shed. Most of the goats went willingly enough back into the original paddock, and from there her father moved them into the milk shed's 'waiting room'. Her mother drove a few stragglers towards Dad, and Tiffany opted to check the dam. As she moved in that direction, Jack strode across the paddock towards her.

She drew a slow, choked breath, and a wave of fresh hurt crashed over her. In control? Holding herself together? Right now it didn't feel like it. She was flying apart one piece at a time, and she didn't know how to stop the process.

He doesn't want you. You tried to connect

and he rejected your efforts. Your friendship is on the rocks, too, and if he hasn't already realised that, he will soon.

So focus your energy on holding onto your pride until he's gone.

Her heart cried out in loss, despite all her attempts not to feel that way. Love for him bubbled inside her, the same way anger had just days ago. It felt like a lifetime. Only this time she couldn't allow that feeling to escape, to reveal itself.

As Jack came to her side she took one last look at him. He was so beautiful. Everything about him, from the defensive, frustrated, hurting scowl on his face to the borrowed gumboots on his feet, made her want to walk forward, right into his arms, and demand he deal with whatever caused him to hold back from her.

Weren't they worth fighting for?

But he'd made it clear they weren't. His 'worst concern' — that he might echo Samuel's behaviour in a close, committed, intimate relationship — was resolved, and all it had done was to drive him farther away from her.

He gestured behind her. 'Has anyone checked the dam?'

'I'll do that now.'

Jack gave a sharp nod. 'I'll help you. It

would be dangerous for you to try to rescue any animals from there by yourself.' His words were rough and low. The tone revealed something similar to the torture she felt.

Her heart tried to hope because of that. And because she didn't feel wholly in control of herself.

Tiffany set out at a fast pace towards the dam. She wished he wasn't right about the safety aspect, or that one of her parents had chosen to come with her rather than leave it to Jack to do so. That way he could go now and she could start to get over all this.

As if it would be that simple.

There was one goat at the dam. A familiar goat. Amalthea stood stuck to her haunches in the mud. Here was another being who couldn't seem to let Tiffany get close.

With a soft exhalation, Tiffany waded in anyway. Amalthea didn't exactly have a lot of choice just now.

Jack followed. 'This pet of yours definitely has a penchant for getting herself into trouble.'

'You could say that.' A lot like her owner, really.

I'm in love with you, Jack. What do you think about that?

'I need to get Amalthea out of the mud.'

184

*I need to get control of my feelings some-
how, and right now I can't manage to even
think beyond what this all means. I'm up to
my calves in mud, and I'm in love with you,
Jack. All the way in love. And you're leaving.*

Jack shifted to the other side of the goat.
'We'll have to make a cradle and lift her
straight up.'

'Yes.' A cradle of their arms, joined together beneath the goat's middle. A strong
bond to help Amalthea move beyond her
current difficulties.

Jack gave his help willingly. He had always
stood up for Tiffany, too. She'd thought they
were an equal team of give and take on both
sides. But they weren't. They never had
been.

'Okay. Let's get her out of here.' Tiffany
gritted her teeth and focused on the suck of
the mud against her gumboots, on Amalthea's struggles as they tried to free her. It
was easier than the whirlwind of her
thoughts.

It took three tries before they got the goat
free. By then Tiffany had fallen into the dam
water twice, Jack once. They were both
soaked and spattered in mud, but Amalthea
was free. The goat had made a beeline for
the other goats at the milking shed. It was a
reflection of their states of mind that neither

she nor Jack had even cracked so much as a smile while they floundered around in the muddy water.

'I guess she wasn't in too deep, after all.' Tiffany slogged out of the dam before Jack could offer her a hand or grasp the irony of her comment. Who knew? Maybe Amalthea had even learned to respect the order and safety of the farm's routine now?

For the next five minutes, anyway.

What did Tiffany need to learn? To let Jack go graciously?

The walk back to the house passed in tense silence.

What was he thinking? Did he share any of her reluctance, or would he be glad to escape? Even in the midst of that tension, they reached the farmyard too quickly.

Suddenly overwhelmed again, and fighting emotions she wasn't sure she could control, she cleared her throat. 'I, ah, I should go to the milk shed. See how things are going.'

'Tiff.' For one long moment he gazed at her with all their past in his eyes, with affection and sincerity and regret.

She thought he might yield, then, open his heart to her at last. Instead, his body tensed and his mouth became a grim line.

He drew away from her before he even took a step.

'I would have taken care of you. I would have tried my very best. It's what friends do.' She whispered it, turned her back and walked away. She had no idea a heart could actually *feel* ripped apart. But hers did, as though a vital living piece of her was rent from top to bottom, never to be the same again.

Tiffany didn't see her father detain Jack for what seemed an idle chat. Nor notice her mother's anxious examination as that woman watched her daughter stride into the milking shed with the pain of a deep loss etched on her face.

Colin Campbell asked Jack to speak freely of Tiffany's progress since Ron's unfortunate accident. 'Our girl worries that she won't please us if things go wrong. It's not that way. We love her no matter what. I'd just like to know things haven't been too difficult for her.'

Jack got how much her parents loved her. He wished Tiffany could get it. She was everything. Sweet, beautiful, giving, loving. And tender. Way too tender and vulnerable, so willing to take his burdens onto her own back and be weighted down by them.

Like stones, those burdens would crush her joy, crush the essence of life she had worked so hard to reclaim when she'd finally come to the Campbells and begun to heal from her childhood hurts. One day she would heal from that fully — maybe with the right man at her side.

Jack wasn't that man, and it had taken him way too long to work out his mistake in coming here and trying to reclaim the past. That simply wasn't possible, and right now he didn't know where that left them. Were they finished as friends? How could he bear that, either?

'Tiffany's been great.' He assured her father of it without hesitation. 'Samuel caused some trouble. Before his accident and all that followed, I mean.' He had explained that to Colin earlier. Now he explained how the goats had strayed onto his father's property.

Colin nodded. 'That's my fault. I should have put more work in on the fences before now.'

'I think Tiffany wants to talk to you about that.'

'That will be fine.' Colin rested that capable hand on his shoulder again, and let go.

Colin was a good man. Jack wished he

could be half as much of a person. 'I should get cleaned up.'

He should get out. Not even phone her unless it was completely unavoidable. Then maybe she could move on, apart from him, find someone right for her, someone without all his baggage.

'Take care of yourself, son.' Colin gave him a level examination for a moment, and walked away.

Jack wondered if Tiffany's father would have been so kind if he'd realised how Jack had hurt her. With a leaden heart, he headed to the farmhouse to shower and change. He felt dead inside. Being with Tiffany had made him feel alive, and now that was over.

Yeah, it felt like the best thing that ever happened to you.

He had wanted to show her those feelings. As he gathered his belongings and headed to the shower memories crowded his thoughts, his heart and senses. Tiffany in his arms. So enchanting. So special. His heart ached afresh.

A soft expletive escaped before he stripped and stepped under the shower's warm spray. 'Just get away from temptation, Reid, and don't step back into it ever again.' He had let himself care too much for Tiffany in the wrong ways, but he was only capable of hurting her.

Tiffany was cold and wet and empty. Jack was gone and she was right back where she started. But it hurt even more now.

'I'll get over him. I will!' But she couldn't imagine not thinking about him, not loving him.

Why don't you take a shower at the house, get into my bathrobe and Dad and I will come over for a cuppa in a while?

That was what her mother had said. Tiffany had almost said no, considered slinking off to the cottage to have a good pity party in private, but in the end she'd agreed.

She had things to tell her parents. About cheese production, about the arrangement she wanted to make with her brothers to hire fencing contractors to overhaul all the necessary fencing. Life had to go on. *She* had to go on. And she would, even if her heart was breaking.

'I have to get a grip — not wallow around and let myself feel like hell.' She muttered the words beneath her breath and pushed open the bathroom door.

Warmth and steam. She noticed those first. Then a woodsy, well-known scent. Then movement. Jack's familiar figure revealed in profile as he glanced over a bare shoulder at the door. Not naked — he wore jeans — but *here.* Jack was still here. Not gone as she had assumed.

A flood of crazy relief welled up. Need and awareness followed as she came to terms with his half dressed state, with that wide expanse of bared skin.

All her defences came down. Words came out before she could try to shore them up again. 'You're breathtaking.' She whispered the words, and he was.

And here she stood, dripping yabby-scented dam water all over the floor.

Even so, all she could do was look. At this beautiful man she had known and loved for so long, and had somehow lost, despite the depth of those feelings.

Her mother's bathrobe slipped from her fingers, fell to the floor as she stood and looked at Jack. Looked and looked.

At his golden muscled back, broad shoulders, strong arms. And she felt . . . she felt . . .

'You — you're so . . .' Sculpted, muscled, beautifully shaped and familiar and dear, and she wanted to touch him all over and never stop.

'Tiffany.' He growled out the word as his gaze took in every centimetre of her. His body seemed frozen, but hunger flared, right there in his eyes, where she could see it, despite how awful she must look right now.

Her gaze skimmed those wide shoulders again, moved over the rounded muscles that were echoed in other muscles down his arms.

He stood half-turned towards her, and she drank in his flat ribcage, the edge of his chest. A moan escaped from the back of her throat and her fingers tingled.

Jack seemed to come out of his frozen state with a snap. Every line in his body tensed. 'Get out, Tiffany. Get out of this room right now.' He ground the words at her, said them in such a harsh tone while his eyes ate her up with torture in their depths. 'I didn't plan to see you again. I planned to write to you — e-mail or something.'

'To say we can't keep seeing each other, even as friends?' If she hadn't seen his pain, she would have bolted. But it was there.

So much pain in him. And she couldn't obey his warning. Instead, she took another step forward. Towards him. Her hands reached out; her heart opened wide. How could she stop it? She couldn't. There was no way.

'Why do you want me out of this room, Jack?'

'Just *go*, Tiff. Now.' Agonised words, clenched fists.

She didn't go. Instead, she stepped in front of him, faced him full-on. 'No. I won't go.'

He made a forbidding, negative sound.

Her gaze dropped from his face to his body.

'No.' His hand clasped her shoulder in a hard grip, ready to turn her aside. But it was too late.

Too late.

Because she'd seen, and hurt gripped her insides and threatened to buckle her knees. A soft gasp ripped from her throat as she took in the hard evidence of his ordeal and realised she hadn't been ready. Nowhere near it.

'This is wrong. This is so *wrong.*' The echo whispered out of her as wrenching heartache scored a path from sight, to mind, to heart. In theory, she had known, but she hadn't realised the damage would be this extensive. The reality of his wounds spelled out every bit of pain and suffering he must have experienced in his fight for life.

A long thin scar ran across the top of his left side rib area and disappeared in a curve up under his arm. There was tissue missing above, a substantial amount — muscle, nipple. His chest hair grew unevenly over a too smooth, too flat expanse of skin that led to the tight scar-line.

Without realising she did it, she took another step backward. His hand dropped away from her. She wanted so desperately to cry, and she couldn't let that happen. If she did, he would never forgive her.

'Ugly, isn't it?' Jack grated the words in a voice unrecognisable in its anguish.

In seconds he'd shrugged into a shirt. He buttoned it with shaking fingers and stared at her, his mouth tight, and she wanted to lift her head to the skies and shout at God that this was so unfair.

'I asked you to leave the room, Tiffany.' His voice held such deep, harsh pain that it seemed to lash out at her. 'You shouldn't have seen this. It's not your business. *It's mine.* Do you understand?'

Yes. She understood now that his hurt went far deeper than she had even imagined. And that he was only uncovering the depth of that hurt now. She had set that response off in him. She felt sick. Should she be proud that she had caused him even more heartache? Easy to stand on the outside looking in and have all the answers, wasn't it?

'I didn't know you were in here.' Her words wobbled. She tried again. 'I apologise. It wasn't intended.' Yet she had pushed at him, tried to use his desire for her to get him to show her his pain. As though she had the right to look at it and tell him to get over himself.

Take off your shirt. Let me see this scar that doesn't bother you.

How could she have said that to him? She felt petty and self-interested, and deeply ashamed of her lack of respect towards his private hurt.

Dull heat rose in her face and she turned her head. She couldn't meet his gaze. 'I'm sorry. I'm so sorry.'

'Yeah. I figure you are.' He made a harsh sound.

She clenched her fists, because if she reached for him now and he pushed her away she didn't know what she would do — and he had every right to reject her, didn't he? Even more so now, in the face of her blundering in on him like this.

Jack glared at Tiffany and cursed the luck that had made her barge into the bathroom just now.

He hadn't wanted her to see his wound,

and he didn't want her to know how much it had hurt him to watch her recoil from the sight.

All the bitterness and anger he'd pushed away over the past months welled up in a choking tide, forced its way forward to where he couldn't ignore it or pretend it away any longer.

Because he did get short changed, and he did resent that. Losing Tiff was the worst of all of it. By far the worst. She was right. He hadn't completely come to terms with all that had happened to him. He hadn't realised that until now. But it didn't matter anyway, did it? Because it was all too late.

He ached for her. He'd never stopped. And he still did, even in the face of her horrified reaction to the sight of his wound. Jack had denied his ongoing need for her, a need that was about something way deeper than friendship. Had he thought he was only a bit in lust with her or something? That showed how truly stupid he had been, didn't it?

Well, he'd covered the scar and the mangled flesh with his shirt. He couldn't do anything about losing her. She deserved better than worrying about him. Right now, she looked as though she would like to run from the room. She was probably relieved that he'd left all those months ago, and that he'd put a stop to that almost lovemaking when they'd escaped the first rain storm.

Tiffany had wanted him to talk, to spill his guts. But he couldn't discuss how he'd felt when he had got his diagnosis. The frustration and fury and fear, and over it all such *loss* as he'd accepted that the devastating news changed everything. He hadn't been able to fully think it, so he'd pushed it all down.

That night he'd gone to her cottage, seen all he had to let go of, and felt such futility because of his family history and his illness and everything else that raised such a wall between them.

So he'd muttered excuses and walked away. The only thing he'd done right was to take care to protect her from all the stress and ugliness that had followed.

All he could do now was protect her again.

'You don't want this, Tiff, and you shouldn't have to face it.' If a part of him wished she could at least have accepted the sight of him, he told himself to get over it.

Why should she manage that when he struggled with it every day and hadn't even admitted the fact until now?

'You should never have seen, known —'

'Well, I *have* seen.' Her face was chalk-white and she swallowed hard. 'Please tell me again, Jack. You won't get sick a second time? You won't have to go through this again?'

At her concern, his heart cracked. Even unable to accept the evidence of his battle, she needed to know he was well.

She'd worry every day that it would come back if you let her that close. You know she would. It would be even more real to her now that she's seen the damage.

If it did recur, she'd have to face the treatment with him. Day after day, week after week, of worry and uncertainty and struggle, and then the long climb back.

Just as she had struggled as a child, and finally escaped that struggle and had to rebuild her happiness in her new family.

Jack had watched that daily struggle on her part. He couldn't and wouldn't ask her to ever go there again. She wasn't over it even now.

'There's no reason to think the disease will come back, but if it did . . .' He drew a sharp breath. If it came back, he could no more ask her to involve herself in his second fight than he would have asked her to step into the first. 'I would handle it.'

'By yourself.' Her hands fisted on her hips as she stood there with her damp hair curled around her face and over her shoulders, mud spatters over her shirt and jeans.

She smelt of sludge, and faintly of goat, and even now his body reacted to the sight of her, to her nearness. She was the most beautiful thing in his life. In the midst of revealing all the opposites of beauty about himself, Jack felt that knowledge to the depths of his heart.

Tiffany's body trembled. Her gaze moved again to his chest, covered now with his shirt, but in her mind's eye was she seeing it all again? The disfiguration and ugliness?

'I can't do this. I can't face . . .' She shook her head, turned away from him.

Jack couldn't look at her any longer, either. He hurt too much.

He lifted his travel bag from the floor. 'I have to go, Tiff. Goodbye.'

He stepped past her and walked away.

CHAPTER TEN

Her parents carried on a conversation, expressed their pleasure about the freshly painted house. Tiffany probably even joined in. But she couldn't feel or really hear, couldn't function beyond her shock.

She sat for long minutes in total numbness at Mum and Dad's kitchen table after her mother had shooed her off to shower and change, before she could even begin to come to terms with what she had seen and the fact that Jack was gone.

Minutes more passed before she got up, muttered some excuse, and walked past her suddenly silent parents and out of the house. Then and only then did shock begin to make way for hurt. Hurt for Jack, and anger for him and *at* him for keeping her at arms' length when she could have been there for him. It wounded her even more now that she had seen *his wounds.*

She didn't have the right to be angry,

probably, but she was. Maybe because she could express that, and everything else seemed locked away so deep down all she could do was feel the pain but not in any way treat it.

So she let rage have its way. She stepped into her kitchen and banged pots and pans about in a fury she could barely explain. Didn't they say cooking was good therapy? Whatever it was that she cooked, she couldn't have said. She scraped it all out. How could she eat when her best friend had faced such a devastating threat and hadn't allowed her to even *know* about it, and even now wouldn't let her near?

All that day her emotions whirled and roiled while thoughts and counter-thoughts, wild plans and furious pain, all rattled around inside her. When the anger dissipated it got harder. And then, when her feelings really started to surface, it got harder still.

Late in the day, as she worked with her mother in the dairy, Mum asked if she was okay.

Tiffany lifted her head and searched the kind, loving eyes that even now searched hers. 'You know, don't you? All of it? That I love him. That he's gone for good? He kept something terrible from me, Mum. I don't understand how he could have done that.'

Her mother didn't ask for an explanation. She simply wrapped Tiffany in a strong hug and held on until Tiff was ready to let go. Only then did she speak, with kindness and compassion in her gaze and tone. 'I would have sworn he loves you, too. It's been there in his eyes for a long time. It's there even more now.'

That was all they said, but late that night, as Tiffany lay in bed and all that had happened finally began to coalesce into something other than confusion in her mind, she knew she had to see Jack just one more time.

She had to look into his eyes and tell him he should not have shut her out of his life when he'd needed her to be in it the most. That she didn't want him to shut her out now, either.

All the secrets were out. If he loved her he would let her in. Maybe his response would hurt even more, but she couldn't leave it at this. She just couldn't.

He'd already received one phone report from his father's foreman, and one from Dr Fennessy. If either of them thought his sudden departure odd, they hadn't said so. Things were under control.

Jack should be grateful to be back in his

apartment. Yet the two-bedroom flat felt barren. As far from warm as a place could get.

Tiffany's cottage was a home. Soft and welcoming, old and a bit tired around the edges, and with soot now ground into the lounge room that might never come out, thanks to her nocturnal visitor. It was a home because she was part of it.

He remembered the feel of her in his arms that night the possum broke in, the weight of her body wrapped around his. Would it ever get any better? This aching need for her that just didn't want to quit?

You left. She saw what you are now and let you leave, and it's what you wanted. You have to let it go.

He paced the too-perfect-and-neat carpet and glared at the slate leather lounge suite. 'I don't like this place. There's no air. No country sounds. No goats breaking through fences.'

His mouth tightened. 'There's no Tiffany, and we're right back where we were. No contact, no closeness, and I hate it.'

There. He'd admitted it. He'd only been gone a day, and he missed her now more than ever before. Even though he now knew she couldn't bear the sight of his scarring.

If his hair had been longer Jack would

have pulled at it. Instead, he rammed his hand over the short mass.

The doorbell sounded. Aching, resentful, lost, he opened the door, then stilled, suspended in shock. 'Tiffany?'

'Yes. It's me. May — may I come in?'

He stepped back, let her step inside, then closed the door after her. 'Why are you here?'

As her presence filled the place, suddenly it didn't seem so cold. He drew an unsteady breath, and probably would have lingered in the small foyer if Tiff hadn't already walked into his living room and whirled about to face him.

She wore a long, flowery sleeveless dress with wide straps and a square neckline, and she had a determined scowl on her face.

Nervous tension created sharp lines around her mouth, and she clasped her hands together as though afraid they would shake if she loosened her grip.

His heart leapt with a hope he mustn't let himself feel.

Caution battled its way upward, as well. If she was here out of some kind of pity . . .

'I wasn't finished with our conversation yesterday.' She crossed her arms over her middle and tilted up her chin in a show of bravado that didn't quite reach the soft, trembling mouth. 'You see, I have a right to some answers — acceptable answers. So far you haven't given me any. Not for your rejection of me when you discovered you were ill. Not for the way you pushed me out of your life when you needed me.'

Her voice lowered. 'Not for refusing to make love with me when that would have meant so much.'

Oh, dear God. He clamped his arms against his sides. His whole body trembled with the need to hold her. She wanted answers? Explanations? And then what?

Then she'll leave. Don't for a moment imagine anything else. She has to leave.

'I gave you the only answers there are.' He ground the words out, felt his composure begin to crack even as he fought to hold on to it. 'I had cancer. I got treatment. Even if I hadn't believed there was a threat of violent rages in me, it wasn't right to ask you to be part of that. You'd have worried too much, carried it and made yourself hurt because of it.'

'And you thought you should continue on with that attitude afterward? Against the possibility that you might have to go through further treatment if the cancer happened to return? You've taken care of your father's needs, but what about us?' She made it

205

sound like a condemnation of his character, rather than a sensible outlook chosen for her sake.

'I did it for you. Because it would have been too difficult for you. You wouldn't have coped. I told you. Your mother —'

'Didn't look after me properly. And, yes, I admit I've allowed that to have more of an impact on my life than I should have, but I had a long talk with my *real* parents about that before I came here, and I don't intend to be like that in the future.' She looked stiff and angry, hurt and uncertain. 'It still should have been my choice to stand by you. You had to let me choose to be with you or not.'

She clamped her hands at her sides. 'We said we'd always be there for each other. We made a solemn pact together. I know it was when we were children, but, damn you, I thought it meant something all the way through our lives. How did we get so far away from that?'

'I treasured our friendship. It did mean something.'

He'd taken her into his heart. Somehow, being with her, growing up with her, had allowed him to turn into something better than his angry father or his remote mother.

'It meant a lot, Tiff. More than I can hope

to tell you.' He grabbed her arms, hauled her up close, and told her with his eyes to believe him.

Their bodies were flush together. He could feel the rapid beat of her heart, see the pulse that fluttered at the base of her neck, could feel her outline beneath the dress where she pressed against him.

He wanted to bury himself in her and stay there until every pain he'd experienced faded from his memory. He wanted to take her pain away, too, and he didn't know how to do that.

She raised her arms. Her hands clenched around his forearms as she glared up at him through a sweep of curly long lashes.

How hard could it be to say the rest? Yet he had to fight to make each word come out. 'Don't you see, Tiff? I didn't know what I was in for, but I knew it would be bad. It was best that I ended it with you before it started. So you had a chance to forget me and find someone else. So you didn't have to be burdened.'

'I didn't want "someone else".' She looked stunned, and still angry, and somehow desolate. 'You just made assumptions about me. And yesterday you left before I had a chance to come to terms with the solid evidence of what has happened to you.' She drew a deep breath. 'There's only one real reason why you kept pushing me away. It's because you didn't want me enough.'

'That's not true.' He burst out with the words.

'Then show me. Make me believe it. Let me be enough for you. Not because I think I have to earn your affection, or anything else, but because *you believe in me.*'

Jack pulled back out of her reach. 'Have you forgotten so much since yesterday?'

Before she could speak, or try to stop him, he pulled his shirt over his head, threw it aside and gestured towards himself. Pride was all he had left as he held her gaze. 'Take a good look, Tiffany. Look at the ugliness of that. You turned away from it yesterday. Well, it's no different today. It's still the same. I'm still just as scarred. I've lost a part of myself that I'll never have back.'

His chest heaved with each breath. 'I pushed you out of my life. Maybe I was wrong about that. I don't know. I don't know anything any more, and just because I want you doesn't mean —'

'Stop.' She lifted her fingers to his mouth, rested them over his lips and closed her eyes.

Tiffany stepped back from him, held his gaze with hers. 'There's only one way.'

Slowly, she bared herself before him, one

piece of clothing at a time, until nothing remained but her in her nakedness and him in his jeans, facing each other.

'I'm stripped and humbled, Jack, so you look at *this*. I want *you,* and I don't care how I look to you. I want you so much I can't think about anything else.'

'Oh, God. I can't —' He caught his breath, moved towards her. His hands closed on her shoulders and he bent his head.

'Show me, Jack. Make me believe.' Her gaze lowered until it rested on his chest. She closed her eyes, reached for him blindly. Pulled his head down to hers. 'I want to make love with you, Jack. Because of our friendship, because of what it could have been, and because of now —'

'I want it, too. More than I've ever wanted anything.' Their kiss became molten instantly, her mouth beneath his and his over hers as every suppressed feeling seemed to well up and spill over.

Jack bit back an anguished sound as desire took over. He wanted only to feel. Not to think, just to experience. It didn't matter that she still couldn't quite look at him, couldn't keep her gaze there.

He focused instead on the sensation of her smooth skin pressed against him. Her softly parted lips allowing him to delve inside, to take what he wanted. And her response, so generous and giving, as she wrapped her arms around his shoulders and pressed into him. As though she couldn't bear to let him go.

Even if it was illusion, Jack chose to hold that knowledge dear. Tenderness crept into his kiss, raised a well of emotion deep inside him as he cradled her close, heartbeat to heartbeat. Who could explain the sense of hope that washed over him?

He couldn't. He only knew that in her arms he somehow found himself again — all the lost parts that had fallen beneath the weight of trying to survive and be without her.

'I want to hold you closer, to be nearer even than this.' He wanted to take her to his bed, and she seemed to understand that, for she raised her gaze to his and the consent was in her expression — a *yes* that reverberated throughout his being until only imperative need remained.

'It's what I want, too.' Only those simple words, but they matched a blaze in the depths of her eyes.

Jack swept her up, into his arms, and carried her to his room, threw back the covers on the bed. He set her head upon his pillow and came down beside her. His arms wrapped around her slender shoulders to draw her close.

Feelings welled up, but he couldn't speak them, and so he buried his face in her hair and breathed in her life and her sweetness, and promised her silently that he would worship her, make this all it could be for her.

She looked deep into his eyes and he tried to hide the churn of emotion, only let her see his pleasure and anticipation.

He lay on his side. She on hers, facing him. She whispered his name, a fierce endearment, and then she lifted herself up, her arm tightened around his shoulder and she pressed her cheek to his chest, to the battered, imperfect, scarred side of his chest.

A choked sound came from his throat. He almost drew back then, but her hand clenched on his shoulder and tenderly, tenderly, she traced the line of his scar with her fingertips. A soft moan escaped him. Of tension, shock, *arousal.*

His body locked into stillness as harsh breaths came one after another from deep within. He'd not been touched there by anyone but a physician for a very long time.

He hadn't known what to expect, what he would feel, but with Tiffany he felt such pleasure.

She pressed her mouth to his flesh, kissed. Her hand drifted from his shoulder to trace the unscarred side of his body while she continued to touch and caress him.

'You're Jack. *My Jack.*' She lifted her head, kissed his collarbone, the side of his neck.

He fell apart there and then in her arms. Felt his heart give way somehow, and a well of emotion flooded through him. When she raised her gaze again he kissed her, a long, hungry, broken kiss that made his desire clear and probably revealed more of his loss of control than he might have wished.

Then she spoke, and he broke apart even more.

'I'm all shivery.' She whispered the confession into his ear. Her breasts pressed against him, and it felt so right, so good, that he rubbed his hands up her back from waist to shoulder, pressed her even closer against him for the sheer pleasure of the feeling.

'You make me shivery, too.' He touched her hair, ran his fingers through the locks and let his palm cup her cheek, and then he hesitated.

'Can you really stand it, Tiff? The sight? Everything?'

'It's not like that.' Her gaze sought his and seemed to hold nothing but truth, sincerity. 'Yesterday . . . it was pain for you, Jack, for the fact that you'd been hurt.'

'All right.' He chose to believe her, as much as he could, and tried to lighten the moment.

He nipped the side of her neck, just because he could, and then had to deal with the effect of her sensual shudder in his arms, and his body's instant demanding reaction to her movement. And he accepted. There would be no lightening of this. Simply none.

'Oh, Jack.' Her breathing turned choppy and her arms tightened where they were locked around his neck.

'I've missed you, Tiff. I've missed *us,* in all sorts of ways.' As he looked into her warm, tender gaze, Jack felt he held such a gift. Something so precious he could barely breathe for the tight band of gratitude and awareness and . . . love that squeezed around his heart.

Yes, love. Not simply friendship and affection, but a love so big he wanted only to show her how much he needed her, all she meant to him.

How long had he loved her this way? He couldn't say. A long time. He just hadn't realised, and now he couldn't hold it back.

He wasn't sure she returned those feelings. It was one thing for her to love him.

He'd never doubted that. But to be *in love* with him? Why should she be?

Jack's hands rose from her waist, moved up her narrow ribcage to lightly touch the sides of her breasts. He let his heart accept the truth of his feelings. He did love her, completely and utterly. Enough that he wanted the chance to put that love into action, to give it to her in these shared moments.

Not even an inner demand to be noble could stop this now. He needed her so much. They'd come too far.

He removed the rest of his clothes without conscious awareness, never dropping his gaze from hers as he rejoined her, held onto her because if he let go he thought he might die.

Shaken, desperate, defences shattered, Jack crushed her to him and forgot everything but the need to claim her.

They couldn't go back now. Tiffany hugged that knowledge to her. Jack wanted this. He did.

'This is right for us.' Oh, how she wanted him to believe that. Not only now, but for ever.

'I want to make this special for you. Nothing has ever mattered to me as much.' Jack whispered the words with such awe and tenderness, and tears pricked at the backs of her eyes.

'It can be special for both of us, together.' She blinked the tears back. Wouldn't let them intrude on this moment, not even if a part of her was afraid, so desperately aware of all the love she felt for him. But she spoke, gave her words to the moment. 'Set me on fire, Jack. Make me burn in a way only you can.'

'Tiff. Baby.' His hands cupped her face and his mouth captured hers and a flood of emotion poured through her.

A deep blue gaze met hers, burned for her, let her in at last — or so in her heart she believed.

'We're here together.' She whispered it because it was her world right now. *Jack* was her world, right now, and she loved him.

He dipped his head and began to kiss her — every part of her. 'Tiffany. Don't let me hurt you.'

She understood. It was inevitable he would know he was her first. She set aside any thoughts about the past experiences he might have had, and simply accepted. This. All she wanted with him and wanted to give to him. Passing that final threshold of trust with Jack was right on both sides, for him and for her. She cared only for that truth.

'You won't hurt me.'

He proved her trust in that truth as he led her into a world of sensation, led her away. When he entered her, a choked sound was wrenched from him. She wrapped her body around him then, reached out in her heart for the depths of him, for his spirit and all the places he ached and hurt.

Let me heal your loneliness and need. Let me be that for you.

'*Jack.*' A single tear leached from her eye.

He kissed it away while he loved her with his body, worshipped her with his gaze. He trembled in her arms and joy burst through her.

This was right. This was so completely and utterly right.

'We're here, Tiff.' His mouth pressed against hers, as though he had to have her lips. 'We're here together.'

'Yes.' She drew a long, shuddery breath. 'Yes. I'm so glad.'

Did love shine in her eyes? If it did, she gave it to him freely as his friend, as his lover.

Jack buried his face in her hair and she thought she heard him whisper.

I love you, Tiff. I love you and I always will.

But that was her heart dreaming up

dreams, and she couldn't bear to do that. Then she put even that thought aside, and gave herself over to a world that drew in just the two of them. This was her world, all she had ever imagined, and she never wanted it to end.

They climbed the pinnacle together, and toppled over with their arms locked about each other and their hearts thundering.

I love you so much.

She'd risked everything. Now she lay in his arms and knew she couldn't have done anything else.

Jack had made no promises, yet she wanted those promises. She rose up on her elbows, searched the depths of his slumberous blue eyes.

You have to let me in for good, Jack. If you can't, then this one moment is all we can ever be.

Emotion welled inside her.

I love you, Jack. I love you with everything I am, and I want you to say that's enough for you.

With their gazes locked, she raised her hand to his chest.

He made a harsh sound in his throat and for a short moment his arms clamped around her, locked her close. She thought she'd won through. Won through properly, finally, for all time. She glanced up at him.

His mouth was tight. Too tight. He swallowed once, and again. His hands rose to her shoulders, closed over her flesh as his eyelids closed. A harsh moan of sound escaped him.

And he turned his head away.

She looked at his profile and her heart broke.

After everything, she'd still lost. He couldn't accept what she so desperately wanted to give him. Her unstinting love and acceptance. Even after all this, Jack couldn't reach for that with her.

A harsh sob welled up and she turned away from him. Silent tears fell, emotion battered her, and after long, still moments, a troubled slumber sucked her down and swallowed her.

She didn't feel it when Jack's arms closed around her and he gave a shaken, broken sigh into her hair.

And Jack slept, too.

CHAPTER ELEVEN

Tiffany woke before dawn with her head on Jack's shoulder, their bodies pressed close. In sleep she must have gravitated to him, unable to hold onto the shreds of composure that demanded she reach this final place of ending with some dignity intact. For it *was* the end. His ultimate rejection last night had made that clear.

For a long time she lay there and took in the feel of his arm around her — the feeling of acceptance and rightness. Even if it was only in her imagination, in her hopes and in her mind.

And in her heart.

She had given herself over to Jack in increments over such a long time. She hadn't realised she could love him more, but last night had proved that, and now her heart clenched. She couldn't stay here and face him — let him send her away, say thanks, but no thanks, break her heart all over again. It wasn't a coward's decision, it was smart. Maybe the only smart thing she had done.

The heartache was there now — deep, unbearable — and she had to find some way to pull herself together and go on.

Without him. Because he'd rejected that final overture, had blocked her out despite everything.

She slipped from the bed, washed and dressed in his bathroom. But she didn't manage to slip right away. As she moved towards the apartment's outer door, she heard a movement behind her.

'You're up.' Jack had a morning voice, gravelly and deep. Even that squeezed at her heart, because she wanted to hear that rough grumble every morning.

In fact, she wanted to crawl back into his bed and make love with him again. Forget everything else and just concentrate on what he made her feel, on how they were together.

But Jack was no longer in the bed. He leaned in the doorway of the bedroom, dressed in boxers and a T-shirt. This was true pain and she had to deal with it.

'I didn't mean to wake you.'

'I figured that.' His mouth tightened. His whole body was coiled with tension. 'Tiff —'

'I have to go.' Why put them through more of this?

He didn't love her — not really, not enough — and nothing she did would change that. She knew that now.

'I'm going back to the farm, and to working at Fred's Fotos and my wildlife treks. I'll move on, Jack. I'll move on, and I won't think about you or care about you ever again. That's what you want, isn't it?'

She rushed from the apartment and out of his life.

Jack had thought he could live with pain, live through it. Two days after Tiffany left, he was no longer certain of that.

He sent her an e-mail.

There could be a baby. I didn't protect you.

Her response arrived the next day.

My period's due any day. I can protect myself and anyone else.

Where had they gone wrong? He had let her in, and she'd made love with him as though it meant as much to her as it did to him. He'd choked on emotion, felt utterly

221

unmanned as he tried to pull himself to-gether. Then he'd slept with her in his arms and felt life was a wonderful gift again, instead of a day-to-day loneliness that had to be endured.

He had made up his mind. He would ask her to stay with him, to share whatever life might bring. She was stronger than he had given her credit for and he would tell her — ask her to forgive him.

Then she had walked away.

A day later she e-mailed him again.

There's no baby.

He told himself this sick, horrible feeling was how he'd felt from the moment Tiffany had left his apartment, rejected him. Hear-ing her news didn't necessarily make it any worse. He'd fooled himself. He couldn't commit to being a parent. No more than he could commit to her. He *didn't* have enough to give. In the end she had made that clear.

He didn't even know if he *could* get her pregnant, anyway. They'd told him it shouldn't be a problem, but who knew for sure?

Who knew how much of life he had ahead of him, either? Scores of years? Or a great many less than that? He didn't have those answers.

After days spent pacing his apartment as he thought about her, longed for her, Jack knew he had to pull himself together. Good reports continued to come in about Samuel, but Jack needed more. He contacted his offices and went back to work. He took up a caseload and looked after his clients as he should have. And he missed Tiffany.

Every day, every night, with a burning desperation that seemed to take over more and more of his heart as the days passed.

Nothing felt right. *Being apart from her didn't feel right.*

Jack toasted that thought with lukewarm coffee on Saturday morning as he stared out at the city skyscape through his closed balcony doors. He couldn't even summon the enthusiasm to sit out there.

'I'm empty. I love her and want her and need her so much, and I don't know what to do.'

Finally he had admitted it aloud. He was confused, couldn't sort his feelings out. He just wanted to hold her and say he was sorry. For everything. He wanted to tell her they could try to make a baby if she wanted to, but he didn't know if she wanted one, and that hadn't even been the point — not really.

Yet Jack wanted to have a child with her if he could. He wanted to make a family with her, make a commitment and never leave her, no matter what. His fingers moved to touch the scarred outline beneath his shirt.

'I miss you, Tiff. So much.'

He'd protected her, avoided her, made love to her, fallen for her. He had wanted to save her from his worries. He admitted now that his reasoning hadn't been fair to her in that.

The deeper truth was that he had wanted to protect himself from the possible hurt of her rejecting him. Because of his scarring, because he no longer had as much to offer her. Because he *had* felt less, just as Samuel had sensed that day.

Jack had been in denial about a lot of things, just as she'd said he was. Yet she had loved him so generously, with such truth in her eyes.

Had touched and caressed his wounds as though she treasured that part of him, as well.

You expected her to reject you, to find fault with your scars and back away, to keep her distance as your mother has all her life, to not be able to love you, just as you thought Samuel never did. Even after she bared herself to you, physically, emotionally, you still expected

224

that of Tiffany.

Well, Jack was watching over both parents from a distance. His mother was still out of the way, which was best for now, and his father responding with some success to a course of treatment he should have received decades ago. Eileen would continue to be selfish, and Samuel might continue to dislike Jack. It didn't really even matter, provided Jack did what he could for them.

But Jack was scarred inside and out for all sorts of reasons that didn't have anything to do with either of his parents. Tiffany wouldn't exactly get a bargain. Yet now that he'd let her go Jack realised how much he wanted and needed her.

Could they have had a together? If he had let her be strong for him as she'd wanted to be? Oh, God. Had he lost her when he'd let her walk away this final time? Caught up in insecurity, had he even . . . *misread* her choice to leave?

He had given her no words of commitment. He'd meant to, wanted to, but emotion had overcome him, and then they'd slept, and then she'd got up and left.

When someone pounded on his outer door, Jack's heart pounded, too. Had she come back to him?

Why should she? All you've done is push

her away, again and again.

His behaviour really was enough to kill off whatever love she might have felt for him. He'd *made love* to her. But there were so many things he needed to say to her. He needed to put things to rights and hope she could accept the offer of his love.

Jack opened the door, but it wasn't Tiffany who stood on the other side. Even as he came to grips with a blast of fierce disappointment Tiffany's eldest brother pushed his way inside.

'Come on in, why don't you?' Jack mumbled it beneath his breath as Cain shoved his way into the apartment.

'I'd like to knock you to the floor.' His friend levelled his gaze at Jack.

That gaze was angry and accusing and . . . pitying?

'Tiffany told you?' Jack stopped. He didn't believe Tiffany would have talked about anything they'd shared during those wonderful moments of lovemaking, about his scarring or its cause.

'She told me she's sure you love her, but not enough, and that you won't keep her.' One of Cain's fists clenched. 'What's with that, Jack? Because my sister is the best thing that ever happened to you or will happen to you, and if she loves you, you should love her back.'

'I know. I've realised.' Realised he had been a total fool and he had to convince her to give him another chance! 'I need to go to her, ask her to forgive —'

'My sister's lost weight, Jack.' Cain bit the words out at him. 'She's pale and looks haunted and I'm worried about her.' Cain didn't wait for a response. His brows drew down and he went on the attack again. 'I figure you're the reason for her distress. I also figure I'll either make you fix whatever ails her, or I'll walk out of here with some of your face on my knuckles — even if you are my friend.'

Tiffany pale? Losing weight? 'She said she wasn't pregnant.' The words escaped because Jack wasn't thinking about the likelihood that Cain might make a knuckle sandwich out of him.

He was taking in Cain's words, words that quickly catapulted him from uncertainty to panic.

Serious illness could manifest itself in weight loss, although it hadn't had time to do so to him before he'd got his diagnosis. What if she was . . . ill? He had to see her, check for himself that she was okay!

'How could my sister run the risk of pregnancy by *you?*' Cain shoved his face into Jack's face. 'For that to happen you would have had to —'

'That's right.' He refused to apologise for something he would cherish for the rest of his life. All Jack could see was Tiffany. 'I have to go to her.'

He had to go, and once he got there he had to tell her he loved her. Even if it was too late for her to love him back.

Whatever else Cain asked or said, Jack didn't hear it. He threw together an overnight bag, got his wallet and keys and walked out, climbed into his Jeep and drove away.

If her brother trailed him to the farm and got in the way Jack would have to deal with that, too. And he would. Nothing would stop him from getting to Tiffany.

Tiffany talked to her goat goddess, poured out her woes into an ear that seemed a little less unfriendly lately. Perhaps the goat, too, had been crossed in love?

'You don't have to be my pet, Amalthea. I'll release you so you can spend all your time with the other goats. I'll never make another demand on your emotions. I won't try to force you to love me. I won't.'

Amalthea butted her head against Tiffany's arm. The gesture was almost kindly, really, in an 'I'm a goddess and you're just a silly human' sort of way.

'I've put him out of my heart, you know.' Tiffany confided her words to the goat and nodded her head for emphasis, ignoring the sting behind her eyelids that belied her statement. 'Not enough time has passed yet, so I still feel a bit raw, but I'm getting there.'

Maybe in another hundred years or so she would actually get rid of the horrid ache inside her and start to feel like a living, breathing part of the world again. Maybe. 'It's just that I loved him so much and he hurt me. He really hurt me, Amalthea. Because in the end he just couldn't love me enough.'

They were in the yard outside her cottage. When Tiffany heard a vehicle approach along the track, she assumed it was her father — or Cain — who had turned up yesterday unexpectedly and then disappeared again just as suddenly to go who knew where? She didn't look up.

It could be Mum, too, come to pick some of the figs from the tree at the edge of the yard. They would talk about fig jam, and Tiffany would pretend everything was all right.

'Tiffany?' Jack stood before her, a fitted green T-shirt stretched over his upper torso, jeans covering his long legs. She registered these small facts as she stared up at him, speechless, and tried to comprehend his presence.

She hadn't expected to see him, and couldn't quite hide her gasp as she rose to her feet to stare at him.

Amalthea made a small sound, and Tiffany tapped her on the rump to send her back up the track towards the farmhouse. Her father was at work in the yard there. He would let the goat into the paddock with the others.

Halfway up the track the goat hesitated and looked back, almost as though to assess whether she should go or stay. Then, with a soft bleat and a nod of a goddessy head, she went on.

Tiffany looked at Jack. 'Why are you here?' She searched his face, examined him carefully, because she couldn't help it. He looked unhappy. Strained. Just as she felt.

'I kept thinking about you all the time. Day and night until I thought I'd go insane. It never got any better. And then Cain came and said you looked unwell.' The words rushed out of him and a sharp blue gaze travelled over her, examined every inch as though he, too, couldn't help caring.

'My brother shouldn't have told you

anything about me.' Tiffany turned away and went inside to the kitchen, where she could put the kettle on and act as though she had some semblance of control over her galloping heart-rate.

Over the almost overwhelming feeling of hope that rose in her because Jack was here. Jack had worried about her.

Only because Cain had interfered where he shouldn't have.

Jack followed her inside and shut the door. 'You said you weren't pregnant.'

'I wasn't. I'm not.' That had made her sad, the day she'd got her period, even though she'd known all along it would come. The timing hadn't been right, and somehow even that had been painfully fitting. 'I sent you an e-mail.'

Was that the reason for Jack's presence? Had Cain's visit somehow made him believe her to be pregnant? That didn't make sense — but she would tell Cain later that he should have stayed away from Jack.

'Yes, you sent me an e-mail.' He looked her over again and didn't seem in any way reassured.

She wished she'd worn a different pair of jeans. These ones were baggy, and they had goat hair on them. She didn't want to tell Jack she couldn't seem to eat well lately, because then he might guess she'd pined for him and feel sorry for her, pity her.

No. Tiffany would not be pitied by Jack. But that didn't stop her wanting to be loved by him, even as she fought it.

'I want you to see a doctor, get checked over to make sure you're okay.' He stepped forward and gripped her arms, and she felt the tremble in his fingers.

'I'm not sick, Jack. Truly. If Cain suggested I was, he shouldn't have.'

Yet Jack thought it was fine to come to her if he thought she was ill?

What about letting her care about him when *he* was ill?

Jack's fingers tightened. 'How can you be sure? You don't look yourself. There are shadows under your eyes, your face is pale. You're thinner.'

He wouldn't let go of this until he was satisfied. Her control cracked a little and she thought: *so what?* Why not tell him? How could it make any of this worse? 'I'm perfectly well as far as I know, Jack.'

She broke out of his hold and stepped backwards, a pace away from him. Then she opened her mouth and let all her hurt pour out. 'I'm simply trying to get over losing the man I love. Because that man turned his back on me and didn't let me care for him

232

and share his burden when he needed that. And even after I gave all of myself to him, my love still wasn't enough.'

On a deep breath she cautioned herself about going on, but couldn't stop. 'You couldn't bear for me to touch your scarring, to look at you and love that part of you, even after all we shared.'

'Is that what you believe?' He stared at her with a stunned expression on his face. 'The way you loved me then — your touch, all of it — meant so much I almost broke down in front of you. I had to fight for control. I thought you realised.'

The words seemed wrung from him. He clenched his hands at his sides, clenched his jaw, but his eyes, oh, those deep blue eyes, were filled with love for her.

Really, truly love? She had to know! 'You didn't hold me, Jack. *I* turned to *you,* in my sleep.'

'No. The moment I felt I had control of myself enough to take you in my arms without . . . crying, I pulled you close. But you'd already fallen asleep.' He swallowed hard. 'I held you all night and didn't ever want to let you go.'

Jack had held her and wanted to keep her always?

'Did you?' A soft, tentative hope filled her.

Then she frowned. 'You have to trust me to love you as you are, too, Jack. You have to understand that seeing your scar caused me anguish because of what you went through. Do you understand that? Do you love me as much as I need you to? Enough that you can trust me when I say you have my heart? Enough to let me be at your side no matter what may happen in your life in the future? I'm strong enough for that. You have to believe it.'

Jack looked at this woman he loved so much, and acknowledged it all came down to this. He had a chance. Tiffany had offered him that. He couldn't believe it, yet the truth was in her eyes. It was in his heart, too.

'I want to be with you for the rest of our lives. As your friend —'

That was just the beginning, but when he spoke those words her face tightened almost imperceptibly, as though in receipt of another blow.

Jack stepped forward then. Took her hands in his and squeezed. 'As your friend *and as your lover.* I want to build on what we had and make it even better. I've never felt what I did when I held you and made love with you. *Never.* But I want to feel it again, with you, over and over.'

He drew her forward until their joined hands rested against his chest. His scarred, imperfect chest, clearly outlined by the fitted shirt he wore. And yet Jack hadn't given it a thought.

All he'd cared about was getting to her, so he could make sure she was all right.

'You need to care for me as much as I need to care for you. I understand that now. And I need you to know *you are enough*, Tiff. You've always been enough.'

The breath he drew wasn't entirely steady. 'I'm sorry I robbed you of the chance to be with me while I faced my operation and treatment.' Words seemed inadequate, but he went on and hoped she would understand. 'You were with me in my heart. Every day. I kept photos of you on my computer, on my bedside table. Longed for you with each moment, each day that passed.'

Tiffany couldn't wait another moment to speak. Oh, how she had missed him. 'I longed for you, too.'

Jack wrapped his arms around her and held tight. 'I tried to protect you from hurt, but instead I hurt you myself. Can you forgive me for that? I love you so much. I'm *in love with you* so much, and I was trying to protect myself, too.'

He stopped to draw a cleansing breath, let

it go at last. 'Even though I denied the thoughts, I worried deep down that you might see me as less of a man, less of a person. You were right about me not facing up to all that had happened. Please say we have a chance, despite the wrong choices I've made in the past.'

'Wrong choices for well-meant reasons. I do understand, and you could never be less to me, Jack. Never in any way.' And he loved her. Really and truly. Oh, her heart soared at that wonderful, longed-for knowledge.

She raised one hand to touch her fingers to his lips. 'If you love me, I can forgive it. Because I love you, too. With all my heart.'

'Then . . .' Jack took a deep breath, held that breath as his gaze locked with hers, and all his love for her shone there for her to see. 'If you still want me, Tiff, wounded and uncertain but very, very much in love with you, will you marry me? Make a life with me somewhere? Maybe find a place a reasonable commute from here, and from Sydney, so we can both continue to pursue our work as we are now? I kind of like the idea of a small farmlet with you, maybe a goat or two.'

Tears pricked her eyes then. She couldn't help it. She took a deep, cleansing breath and let the hurt go, all of it. 'Yes, Jack. Yes,

I'll marry you, and live with you wherever we decide is best. You've made me realise I was holding onto the past, to those feelings of inadequacy I thought I'd overcome. I know now it's not about working hard, or doing some special thing to earn love. In the right relationship that love comes naturally, out of the respect and affection and commitment the people have for each other.'

'I couldn't love anyone more than I love you.' He wrapped his arms around her, pulled her in close against his body and groaned as they came together at last. 'My parents are messed up, but I'm keeping an eye on them both, and the doctors have put Samuel on long-term medication to help him control his anger. If my father settles down and Eileen behaves herself, I think they'll be as happy as they can be. But I want more than that with you. Now I know I can have it, I'm overwhelmed.'

When he paused to draw a deep breath, she offered an encouraging smile. 'I feel that way, too.'

'You're my home.' Jack uttered the words in a deep voice filled with gratitude and love. 'Anywhere you are creates that place for me. I've missed being *home,* Tiffany. I've missed it so much.'

'Then show me how you feel. I want to

know it, to be certain of it.'

'I'll make you believe it.' He led her towards her bedroom. 'I'll never let you go.'

At the side of the bed she paused and looked up into his face. 'I know you can't promise to stay well, but I hope you'll never go through anything like that again.'

'I'll have the best reason to want to live, to grow old with the only woman who will ever hold my heart.' He hesitated. 'I asked you about getting pregnant, but there's a chance that won't be able to happen.'

'I wondered as much.' She didn't even blink. 'Mum and Dad have shown that a family can be a lot more than a biological child and its parents. If we want children and can't have them, we can foster or adopt, too. Or we'll simply have each other — whatever is right for us.'

She cupped his face, leaned in close and let their lips brush, and it *was* a homecoming, for her, too. 'I just want *you,* Jack.'

Jack buried his face in her hair and inhaled, a shaken sound yet filled with hope and promise. 'I think it will take me a very long time to show you how much I need and love you.'

She smiled and reached for him, lay her hand over his heart. 'Then perhaps you should start right now.'

ABOUT THE AUTHOR

Australian author **Jennie Adams** grew up in a rambling farmhouse surrounded by books and by people who loved reading them. She decided at a young age to be a writer, but it took many years and a lot of scenic detours before she sat down to pen her first romance novel. Jennie is married, with two adult children, and has worked in a number of careers and voluntary positions, including transcription typist and preschool assistant. Jennie makes her home in a small inland city in New South Wales. In her leisure time she loves taking long walks, starting knitting projects that she rarely finishes, chatting with friends, going to the movies and new dining experiences.

Jennie loves to hear from her readers, and can be contacted via her Web site at www .jennieadams.net.

We hope you have enjoyed this Large Print book. Other Thorndike, Wheeler, and Chivers Press Large Print books are available at your library or directly from the publishers.

For information about current and upcoming titles, please call or write, without obligation, to:

Publisher
Thorndike Press
295 Kennedy Memorial Drive
Waterville, ME 04901
Tel. (800) 223-1244

or visit our Web site at:

http://gale.cengage.com/thorndike

OR

Chivers Large Print
published by BBC Audiobooks Ltd
St James House, The Square
Lower Bristol Road
Bath BA2 3SB
England
Tel. +44(0) 800 136919
email: bbcaudiobooks@bbc.co.uk
www.bbcaudiobooks.co.uk

All our Large Print titles are designed for easy reading, and all our books are made to last.